SAUCY MOVIE TALES

June 1936

Saucy Movie Tales
June 1936

This reprint edition is a facsmile edition. Variations in print
and quality are mostly attributable to the rough woodpulp
original this reprint edition is based on.

ISBN: 1-59798-008-0

ALSO FROM ADVENTURE HOUSE

FICTION

- **High Adventure**
(more than 80 issues published)

- **G-8 and His Battle Aces**
(more than 15 issues published)

- **At The Stroke of Midnight**

- **It's Raining More Corpses In Chinatown**

- **Roscoes In The Night**

- **Footprints On A Brain**

NON-FICTION

- **Uncovered: The Hidden Art of the Girlie Pulps**

- **Rudolph Belarski: Pulp Art Masters**

- **Pulp Fictioneers**

- **The New Pulpwood Editor**

- **Those Macabre Pulps**

SAUCY MOVIE TALES

Combined with
"Stage and Screen"

VOL. II.   JUNE, 1936   No. 2

CONTENTS

SAUCY MOVIE TALES is published monthly by Movie Digest, Inc., Broadway, New York, N. Y.

Starlight

Events such as these behind Casting Office doors would give the cinema city a black eye!

By KENNETH STALCUP

"MISS CECILY BLACKWOOD'S calling!"

Looking up f r o m the senario upon which he was trying to focus his mind, George Burlington, casting director for the Starlight Films Corporation, scowled irritably.

"I can never get a moment's peace!" he grumbled.

Helen Flood, his secretary, who knew that his bark was much worse than his bite, stood beside his desk with sympathetic understanding.

"Don't blame me!" she retorted with a smile. "I didn't ask the lady to visit you today."

"What does she want?"

"What do all of them want?" said Helen. "An assignment as star of the very next picture we produce! Isn't that the modest demand you get from most of your callers?"

George grabbed his pipe and applied a match to it. Puffing out a cloud of smoke, he asked:

"Who sent her?"

"She's got the usual letter of introduction. . . . Here it is!"

George read the missive and let it fall among the other papers on his littered desk.

"A friend of Mike Andrews," he remarked. "You know what that means, don't you?"

"Just what does it mean?" murmured Helen.

"I've got to see her! Mike's money makes the wheels go around here."

Helen laughed. "Well, I'm glad that *something* makes it possible for us to hold our jobs! Heaven knows it isn't the excellence of the pictures that are turned out in the studio."

George ignored the thrust.

"What does she look like?" he asked.

"Oh, very dark and very dreamy and very vampish!"

George grinned wisely. "Mike would pick a dame like that."

"If you're casting a South Seas picture some time," Helen went on, "you might use her. . . . You know, with scenes where the natives go around with grass fringe about their tummies and little else above or below! Cecily ought to be in the front row in all those shots."

"Good figure, huh?"

"It's a wow, I'm telling you."

"That kind is a weakness of Mike's."

Helen laughed once more. "Don't blame it all on poor Mike. He isn't the only one who is weakminded on the subject of full-bosomed beauty. . . . How about yourself?"

George put down his pipe, and leaned back in his swivel chair.

"Don't get personal. . . . At least, not right now. . . . We've got to fix up Mike's girl friend."

"Shall I send her in?"

"Shoot!" said George.

Helen wafted herself out of his private office, swinging her hips tantalizingly as she walked.

"Hey!" he called out as she reached the door. "You're a swell number for that South Seas picture you were speaking about."

"Not really, Mr. Burlington!" she intoned, tilting her pretty nose in the air and sailing through the doorway.

A FEW moments later, she approached Cecily Blackwood, who was seated expectantly on the edge of a chair in the outer office.

"Mr. Burlington will see you now."

"Oh, thank you *so* much!"

Cecily jumped up quickly and followed Helen down the hall. At the entrance to George's sanctum, the latter stood aside and Cecily went in. Helen watched her walk snakily across the rug in front of his desk, and then she gently closed the door.

"That's that!" she muttered to herself on the way back to her own desk. "But you'd better watch your step, George, old boy! The girl's got what it takes to make you lose your head.

George rose as Cecily advanced to meet him.

"How do you do, Mr. Burlington?" she gushed. "So good of you to grant me an interview!"

"It's a pleasure!" said George. "Won't you sit down?"

"Thanks! I know you must be terribly busy."

Settling herself in an armchair, which she selected because of its location where none of her attractive physical charms would be hidden from the view of the casting director, she slowly crossed her legs, and in doing so allowed a glimpse at intimate territory far above her smooth kneecap.

"What can I do for you?" George asked, as his eyes roamed about her. "By the way, will you have a cigarette?"

She took one, and accepted the light in his outstretched hand. Then she let herself sink back languidly in the chair.

"I was talking with our mutual friend, Mike Andrews, the other day," she began, in a warm, colorful voice, "and he asked me if I had ever been on the stage. . . . I told him that I hadn't. . . . Then he said that I was born to be a movie star!"

George flicked the ashes from his cigarette and waited. He knew that Cecily had simply paused for effect.

"Well, you know Mike!" she continued. "He's *such* a dear! You might think I was conceited if I repeated some of the things he told me. . . . But he said: 'You go and see George Burlington! He'll be glad to assign you to a role in the next Starlight production.' . . . So he scribbled that note of introduction, and here I am!"

Her pretty lips, blood-red, parted in a sugary smile, and the dreamy droop of her eyelashes, called attention to the purple-black orbs which were fastened upon George.

"I'd love to be a movie star!" she breathed fervently.

Extinguishing his cigarette stub, George looked out of the window before replying. . . . He wanted to laugh! . . . How many times had he heard that same ambitious declaration! It seemed to be the one and only idea of thousands of beautiful girls who migrated to Hollywood from every section of the country, seeking to capitalize the sex allure which most of them possessed in heaping measure.

Cecily was one of the most attractive blondes that he had been called upon to interview in his many years of casting experience, and he didn't blame Mike Andrews for trying to make himself solid with her. George had become fairly hardboiled from his daily contact with girls who were willing to "do anything" to get in the movies, but he had to confess to himself that this Cecily person was making a dent upon his inner consciousness, something that most of the yearning beauties failed to do.

Shifting his glance from the window back to the lovely girl who expectantly awaited his verdict, he said:

"I'd be glad to do anything I could for you, Miss Blackwood."

Picking un a pencil, he made a note on a memorandum pad.

"Call me Cecily!" she gurgled. "Let's not be so formal."

"All right, Cecily!" he grinned. "I prefer that name, too. . . . A friend of Mike Andrews is always a friend of mine."

"Isn't he a charming chap?" she smiled.

"He is!" agreed George. . . . Mike had more money than he knew what to do with, plus a personality that gained him admittance to many exclusive boudoirs in Hollywood and Beverly Hills. In addition to a wide and very intimate acquaintance among the feminine galaxy of stars who had already "arrived," he was constantly broadening his sphere of amorous activity to include carefully selected specimens from among those who struggled to get into the favored circle of moviedom, of whom Cecily was one!

"That guy certainly knows how to pick them!" thought George, as his eyes rested upon her soft, slim contours, and the cameo-like beauty of her facial profile, framed by a profusion of blond, wavy hair on which a saucy, close-fitting hat was set at an impertinent angle.

WOULD you mind removing your, eh—" he asked.

"Not at all!" said Cecily blithely, slipping off the garment, a part of her ensemble costume. She said it with the air of one who would not be adverse to discarding *any* portion on request!

The bodice clung to her torso revealingly, and the snow-white hue of her smooth-textured skin, exhibited by her bare arms and neck, was startlingly opposed to the ebony tints of her hair and eyes. Bulging voluptuously under the thin material, a rounded bosom strained in silent but eloquent protest against their confinement.

Cecily knew that her figure was on inspection. . . . She arose from the armchair, walked gracefully to the window, stood there for a few moments in a charming silhouette of face and form, then slowly came back to George's desk and paused, looking down at him.

"I've got a little part in a forthcoming picture that I think you could do very well!" he said, leaning back in his chair.

"I'm *so* glad!" she murmured.

"Of course, you'll have to take a test before I can definitely decide. . . . Do you photograph okay?"

"My friends say I do," declared Cecily. "But I can bring you some photographs of myself taken at home."

"Never mind!" said George. "I'll arrange for a test tomorrow, say at ten o'clock in the morning. . . . How would that suit you?"

"Splendid!" she cried.

"Bring along an evening gown, a couple of negligees and a swimming suit. . . . You would have to wear that sort of thing in the production I've got in mind."

Cecily laughed. "I won't disappoint you, Mr. Burlington."

George nodded wisely. "I don't think you will!" His eyes were wandering about her, here and there, finding so many delightful spots to gaze upon that he couldn't concentrate on any one!

Slipping her arms through the sleeves of the jacket which he held for her, she turned to face him. A haunting fragrance, an enticing mixture of heady perfume that was a combination of odors packed in crystal cut bottles and the sexy warmth of Cecily herself, lingered in his nostrils.

"You've been very kind to me,

Mr. Burlington," she said smilingly.

"Call me George!" he chuckled. "Why should *you* be formal if you permit me to be informal?"

"Fair enough!" she retorted. "I like you a lot, George."

He clasped her hand and squeezed it gently. "You're a sweet little girl! I'll see you at ten o'clock tomorrow. Everything will be ready for your test. . . . Don't oversleep, and go to bed early this evening. . . . The camera isn't kind to tired faces, you know."

"I'll be in bed right after dinner!" she smiled. "But I'm afraid I won't be able to sleep from excitement."

He patted her shoulder as they moved toward the door.

"Take it easy and don't worry!" he advised. "You'll be a big success."

"Bye-bye!" she whispered. "I really don't know how to thank you, George."

"Tut-tut!" he said. "Forget it!"

The door closed gently, but as she vanished that enchanting odor of Cecily-sex-and-perfume m a d e h i m sniff the air repeatedly.

"Phew!" he whistled, walking back to his desk. "Mama, mama, buy me that!"

Passing Helen's desk in the ante-room, Cecily smiled:

"Good-bye!"

Helen also smiled: "Good-bye!" And after the movie-struck blonde had disappeared, the secretarial mind reverted to her boss in the private office.

"I wonder how our efficient casting director survived *that* nice interview?" thought Helen, pushing back her chair.

George was staring like one in a trance at the now empty armchair in which Cecily had draped her beau-teous form a few minutes before, and he didn't hear Helen enter the room.

Her merry laughter aroused him.

"Come back to earth!" she said. "You look like you've been doped or something."

"I've got a lot of things to think about on this job!" he mumbled.

"Oh, yes, lots and lots!" she replied teasingly.

George lighted a cigarette and inhaled deeply.

"You might invite me to have one!" Helen hinted.

"Help yourself!" he said listlessly.

Helen's relationship with George had long since passed the stage of employer and secretary. In fact, it was less than a week after she had been installed as guardian of the outer portals that he had become acutely aware of her blonde attractiveness, and she didn't hesitate to take full advantage of the opportunity for love-making as a thrilling side-line.

NEARLY a year had elapsed since that first torrid outburst late one afternoon, and during that time Helen's soft arms and kiss-thirsty disposition had provided countless periods of hectic diversion for the busy George.

"Did that glorious dame leave you woozy in the head?" she asked, puffing her cigarette and sinking into the armchair that Cecily had just vacated.

"Nonsense!" George snorted.

"Will she do?"

"I might give her a chance! She's got a good personality."

Helen smiled broadly. "I'll say she has! And several other very tempting points besides."

"She's taking a screen test tomorrow," George remarked blandly.

Striking a pose, Helen giggled: "Another blushing violet headed for stardom and her name in twinkling lights!"

"Maybe!"

"And, then again, maybe not!" Helen finished the thought for him. The way she was sitting in the armchair caused her knitted dress to mold itself around her lush curves. Tiny sleeves left most of her creamy-fleshed arms quite bare, and the neckline extended downward like a spearhead to the sharp dividing line between her breasts, which were squeezed together by an affectionate brassiere.

"She says she's going to bed right after dinner, so she'll be fresh tomorrow for her screen test!"

"Alone?" whispered Helen, winking a limpid eye.

"The conversation didn't go that far!" George returned.

"I think it could have gone *much* further."

"Be yourself, girlie, be yourself!"

Helen laughed mischievously. "Ask Mike . . . he'll know!"

Curled up in the armchair, with her legs tucked under her, she was an eye-appealing bundle of blonde charm, soft and luscious.

She was gazing out of the window, but she knew that George's eyes were moving amorously about her. . . . They always did! It was something she could always expect.

Nonchalantly, she disentangled a leg from beneath her and swung it over the arm of the chair in a manner that caused the skirt of her dress to recede almost to the spot on her ivory thigh where her stocking was held securely by a garter clasp.

"Visibility is good!" muttered George. She glanced at him with a flirty smile.

"Could it be improved?" she asked, dangling that leg.

"Getting better all the time!" he commented.

"How's that?" she whispered, squirming so that the swinging limb could describe an ever-widening arc.

"Perfect!" George's murmur of approbation was enthusiastic, as well it might be!

"Come over here!" she invited.

George sidled in beside her on the chair.

"Why do you wear those confounded things?" he asked, fumbling with the clasp of her brassiere.

"Because this is an office, Georgie darling, not a boudoir!" she replied. "Besides, it's thrilling to have you fussing with it."

"What's the correct combination to open the treasure-chest?" he growled.

"Oh, you poor dear!" she laughed. "See?" With a flick of her pink-tipped finger, the brassiere gave way, and then George feasted his eyes upon two cherry-peaked hills of yielding flesh into which his right hand buried itself. At the same instant, his left hand crept along a blue-veined thigh to her dimpled knee.

Meanwhile, her dainty, trembling fingers weren't idle!

Around his neck a soft arm entwined itself, and Helen's lips were fused with his in a kiss of biting, blinding fury!

ON THE following afternoon, Georgie sat in his office studying the results of Cecily's screen test.

"Swell!" he exclaimed.

The poses in evening gown were exquisite. . . . The swimming suit

They took "stills" of her, garbed not only in negligee, but also in bathing suit and undies

pictures were superb. . . . But those in her negligees were so gorgeous that his heart thumped against his ribs in suffocating throbs.

"She'll be a riot in that role!" he muttered. "That is, if the director can make her act like this when he shoots the picture."

Just then Helen put in her appearance.

"Sorry to interrupt your worship at the shrine of the lovely Cecily in pictures," she said sarcastically, "but the fascinating creature is here in person, palpitating to see you!"

George laughed sheepishly.

"I asked her to drop in this afternoon," he said in a careless tone. "Send her in."

"Immediately, your highness, if not sooner!" said Helen, bowing deferentially. Then she added, with an amused glance at George: "Be careful, now! Don't get *too* excited! It's bad for your heart!"

George paid no attention to her gibe. . . . He was looking at a soul-stirring photo of Cecily in a negligee that generously gave a glimpse of nipples that might have been flower-buds, adorning a bosom that was gleaming white marble!

The door opened, and in walked Cecily.

"Good afternoon!" George greeted.

"Hello, Mr. Burlington—George, I mean!" she exclaimed, trying to suppress the emotion in her voice.

"The test was a wonderful success!" he reported.

"*Really?*" she breathed. "How wonderful!"

She peeped over his shoulder. "Can I look at the pictures?"

"Certainly! Sit here."

She took his seat at the desk. "They *are* nice!" she whispered. "I didn't think I could look like this."

A smile lingered on her pretty lips as she let the photos drop, one by one, from her fingers. Then she glanced at the picture in negligee that showed most of her flower-tipped bosom.

"Oh!" she blushed.

George laughed heartily. "Don't mind that!"

"I knew my negligee slipped that time!" she said, joining in the laughter.

"It's the most beautiful picture of all!" said George, bending over her.

"Honest?" She tilted her face upward. Her parted lips were too appetizing for George to resist. Swiftly, his mouth swooped down and kissed. . . . Cecily closed her eyes in passionate response.

"Oh! . . . Oh! . . . Mr. Burlington! . . ." she gasped, as their lips finally separated.

He slipped an arm around her, searching for the living bosom that was so magnetic in the photograph.

Cecily quivered in his embrace. "Oh . . . G-e-o-r-g-e!"

Her voice trailed off into the merest whisper as their mouths once more merged in a welding flash of flame.

Fifteen m i n u t e s later, Cecily tripped through the ante-room.

"Good-bye!" she smiled, passing Helen's desk.

"Good-bye!" said Helen, adding in an undertone as Cecily's back disappeared from view: "I hope you enjoyed your visit!"

George was endeavoring to look unconcerned when Helen approached him. He really cherished a profound respect for the permanency of Helen's affections and regard.

"Don't be a fakir!" she said. "How's your heart?"

"Fine, thanks!"

"I WAS a bit worried!" Laughing, he drew her down on his lap.

"And a little bit jealous, too!" she whispered. "Don't you like me a little?" Helen knew that the casting director regarded her highly.

"Much—much more than that," he replied fervently. "I think you will make a much better wife than a secretary."

She snuggled closer to him. At the touch of her bosom against the firm muscles of his chest, rivers of fire ran through his veins. His lips began swift journeys over the lovely curves and hollows of her body, while his fingers clasped her shapely hand. Temporary, passionate "sex appeal" was one thing; but a permanent, lasting love which forever attracted him, day in and day out, qualified Helen for the mating call.

"Well, George, you took long enough to find it out, darling, and for a casting director, that's a h—l of a black-eye."

Yellow Peril in Hollywood

An Oriental invasion! Hollywood beauties in danger, and "Satan" Devlin to the rescue!

By ERNEST MANNING

"**S**ATAN" DEVLIN, ace cameraman and trouble-shooter for Phoenix Films, Inc., brought his six foot of muscle to a sudden stop outside the All-Nite Restaurant on Hollywood Boulevard, and stared with hard grey eyes ahead of him.

Instinctively he crouched back into the shadows of the restaurant's service alley. He didn't want to be seen—at least not now.

Through his tight, strong lips a muttered exclamation escaped him:

"Darling! Back in Hollywood!"

Yes, it was Grace Darling leaving the restaurant. Dressed in her usual daring provocative style. A style that had caused m o r e rumpus amongst moralists than any Hollywood scandal. She'd caused fits in the Hays' office. A famous New York divine had preached against her.

John "Satan" Devlin could see almost to her waist. For her snowy white ermine jacket was open to reveal bulbous, w h i t e attractive breasts which a silly cobweb of gown scarcely pretended to conceal. He could see right through the silk.

And her skirt wasn't any better. The white fur jacket ended above the seductive curve of a sweet little contour behind. Against the bright lights of the street, her shapely limbs inside the opalescent silk were clear dark shadows. Maddening!

As her high heels twinkled to the limousine waiting at the curb, she turned her beautiful fair head to smile with red lips at her prosperous looking escort.

Prosperous and fleshy was Rangoff Dunn. From the brim of an opera hat, his beady eyes glittered as he returned her smile with a snaky grin of thin lips and followed her into the car.

Sight of Rangoff Dunn fired a charge of fury and horror in Devlin's heart. For he knew that Grace Darling's daring attire was merely a publicity stunt, that she was a decent hard working girl who had suffered bad breaks in the films, and that her return to Hollywood under Dunn's auspices meant only one thing . . . she had promised to pay Dunn's grisly price.

And Dunn was a fiend, shunned by all other movie moguls.

Half in hope of getting the girl out of the car, Satan jumped forward. But the limousine shot away silently . . . leaving him glaring with cold anger after its tail light.

The angry red of its light was no fierier than Satan's eyes when he whirled into the restaurant and called a number in the phone booth by the cashier's desk.

"Publicity Booster's Corporation? Has the Commercial Information Department closed for the night? . . . then give the Celebrity Reporter, please . . . hallo! Has your desk received information of Miss Darling's return from the East?"

"Mr. Rangoff Dunn corroborated the rumor an hour ago," came a metallic voice over the wire.

"Where is she staying?" Satan rapped.

"We don't give out that information over the phone unless the celebrity wishes it."

"Hey—wait—this is John Devlin of Phoenix Films inquiring. I've business with. . . ."

"I'm sorry, we don't—"

"Is Harry Rolf in the office?" Satan snapped.

"Eh? Mr. Rolf. Who's speaking, please?"

"I told you. John Devlin. Get him on the phone."

"Oh, certainly, Mr. Devlin. Pardon me. . . . I'll connect you."

Satan jerked a cigar from the vest while he waited impatiently. Clamping the unlighted cigar he snapped suddenly: "Rolf?"

"Say what you've got to say, quickly, Satan," came a low cultured but hurried voice. "I can't spare a minute. Hell's breaking loose on the wires."

Satan blinked. "What's Grace Darling's address?"

"43, Mirimar Apartments. Is that all you wanted to know?"

"Thanks . . . yes. . . ." Satan responded to curiousity aroused by his normally cool friend's hasty answer. "Say—tell me what's the trouble in your place?"

A moment's hesitation. Then: "We're hoping to avoid any panic in the film industry, Satan. Business as usual and all that sort of thing, you know. So what I say mustn't go any further, do you understand?"

"Sure! Shoot!"

"Okada Huma, naval leader of the Japanese Militarist party, escaped, as you know, sometime ago, the Emperor's firing squad by letting his brother die in his place and smuggling himself out of jail by lying under his dead brother in the coffin. Trans-Pacific cable reports he has gained recontrol of the navy and army. You know what that means!"

Satan's teeth clenched on his cigar. "War, I guess."

"We're hoping against hope, Devlin. But whatever happens, we must keep cool. Business as usual. Actors must act, films must continue grinding. . . ."

"Oh, sure." Satan laughed grimly as he hung up. War! Well, Rolf didn't sound so cool himself. Scared stiff, no doubt. What fools people were! Kept their heads in the sand until danger was biting their tails and then had hysterics. Business as usual! Thousands of actors, cameramen, extras, and the whole trade of a city dependent upon business as usual. He stopped at the cashier's desk for a light to his cigar and swung into the night, aiming for the Mirimar Apartments.

THE Mirimar's largest and most luxurious apartment belonged now to Grace Darling.

Darling wasn't her real name but she liked it and preferred it even to her rightful first name. It fitted her personality. She was a darling, p i q u a n t, delicious, dangerously warm.

The negligee in which she received Satan made her a bundle of delicious loveliness. With s t a r r y eyes she smiled at him, drawing him by her tiny hands, as well as hypnotizing him by the rising hillocks of glorious enticement which frivolously bobbed as she sank onto a couch.

"I was just going to bed—Rangoff Dunn left a moment ago," she giggled. "But I'm so g l a d you dropped in. I've wanted to see you, Satan. How did you find my address. You must be the devil himself—really."

Satan Devlin stood glaring down at her, legs spread apart, hands in pockets. His head jerked forward between his shoulders. His tone was enraged.

"Look here, Darling . . . you don't have to return to films by way of Dunn."

Her liquid eyes shaded: "Don't I?"

"No!"

"Satan" crouched back into the shadows as Grace Darling passed with her escort.

"I can hear you without your shouting." She pouted. "Do you know Dunn is starring me in his next picture. He says it's a perfect vehicle for my personality."

"Any picture of Dunn's is a carriage to hell," he snarled.

"Well, it will get me somewhere," she said with the accent on "some."

"Why don't you try the other studios?"

"I've tried. They won't have me."

"Why not?"

"They're frightened of the moralists. The goody-goodies have their knives into me since I went to the races as Lady Godiva in Patou's new cellophane-chiffon."

HE SWUNG on his heel. "Damn all reformers. But wake up! They'll forget all about you now— about your clothes, I mean. They'll have other things to think about. Maybe we'll have a war."

"War?" she gasped.

"Yes." He went over to her quickly, sank on one knee by her side. "You won't need Dunn, Darling. Break with him now. People will have forgotten all about the scandal of your clothes. You can start afresh."

She allowed his hands to brush against her full provocative breasts. Allowed his eager, trembling fingers to insinuate themselves against the perfumed valley of her negligee. Wriggled as he touched each rigid, swelling pink tip.

"I always liked you, Satan."

"Break with Dunn," he muttered.

"I can't." She opened her lips for him to taste the ineffable sweetness of her. "He has me tied up on contract. Besides, dear, he knows. . . ."

"Knows what?" he panted.

"A little secret about an innocent trip you and I took together to Aqua Caliente when I was new out here. Oh, I know it was all right, but the moralists wouldn't, and if Dunn spread that story right on top of the clothes business, the Hays' office just wouldn't let me play anywhere."

To make up for her decision, she went as far as to flatten against him as he bent over her, to let her soft tummy melt against his hard one, welding her body close.

He drew a deep breath. "Dunn can't prove a thing."

"He has photographs, sweet devil. In his cabinet. He showed me."

"And negatives, too?"

"They're all in the cabinet in his library where he can put his hand on them any time he feels like calling up the newspapers, he says."

Satan was beginning to quiver violently, and to take short rapid breaths. But at this he drew away by a violent effort of will, pushing her soft clinging arms away.

"In his cabinet, eh?"

Her liquid eyes widened in alarm. "Satan—you can never get them. Burglar alarms, guards . . . they're all round his place. Remember that burglar who broke in and got shot. They shoot to kill."

"Two can play at that game," he rasped in a steel-edged tone. "I'll fix Dunn . . . blackmailing you with photos. . . ."

She crouched on the silken couch and jumped into his arms. "No, sweetheart . . . stay here with me . . . don't get into trouble on my account."

He laughed grimly as he determinedly set her down. "No fear of me getting into trouble, Darling. I'm a trouble-shooter—and fixer . . . maybe I can make a little on my own account if it's that necessary."

Darling flushed. "You selfish man. Here I'm ready to be nice to you—and you're running away to bust up my chances with the only picture man who'll hire me."

He quirked his mouth. "Everyone will be wanting to hire you soon. You leave it to me."

She stamped her little foot. "Don't you dare leave me. . . ."

He waved his hand round the open door. "Bye-bye. Be seeing you tomorrow. And get ready to tear up your contract with Dunn."

"I hate you," he heard through the door as he closed it and started for the elevator.

He chuckled softly to himself.

*   *   *   *   *

CLICK! That was one burglar alarm severed.

The moon shone on the silvery tape which was glued to the inside of Dunn's basement windows. The tape was actually silver-foil which would break if a pane of glass was broken, and in breaking disconnect a circuit and so release a trigger that would start a bell ringing.

Satan knew all this well. Also he knew how to drill holes through the window frame at each side, stick through needles joined by an electric wire and so keep the circuit from breaking, while he plastered glued paper to the windowpane and gently pushed his elbow through it.

He was breathing heavily when all this was done and he was tiptoeing across the cold stone floor of the cellar in damp, Stygian darkness.

At the top of the cellar steps he saw the shadow of a sleepy guard slumped in a hall chair—three swift strides on rubber-soled shoes across the polished hall floor and he had the guard breathing deeply of the quick-acting a n a e s t h e t i c, ethyl-chloride. P l a c i n g the saturated handkerchief across t h e guard's mouth, he caught him in his arms and dragged him to the cellar.

The grandfather clock in the hall struck two. Two in the morning and all still and silent. Satan's grim smile remained as he operated on the cabinet lock with skeleton keys. Dunn had trusted too strongly to the guards and the burglar alarms—the lock opened easily.

Satan's brows rose. Photographs there were, but all kinds of photographs. Many girls in all poses—and far more people at races and outside hotels than merely him and Darling. Dunn kept a regular blackmailer's folio. Crumpling and pocketing the photos of Grace and himself, Satan turned to the upper drawer and fiddled a brass wire in its smaller lock.

The lock baffled. He screwed a bradawl into the wood and found it was steel-lined. Something very special in this little drawer. He rubbed his chin, stuck a cigar in his strong firm mouth, and attacked the lock with an instrument of his own invention.

It opened noisily. He pulled it out, glanced at the library door for caution's sake, and then took a peep at the papers and pictures in the little drawer.

"Jumping Jehoshaphat!"

The unlighted cigar fell to the carpet. His hands shook as he held the pictures and papers under the library table lamp.

No women here. Nor men neither. But *battleships!*

Battleships a n d harbors, lighthouses, coast artillery gun emplacements, and transport anchorages!

Charts with fathoms marked, all photographed in small size, reduced to microscopic dimensions, for easy hiding and conveyance.

And on the backs of the photos, marks in Japanese.

He couldn't read them. No need to. They proved Dunn a spy all right.

Spy? Maybe a half-breed Jap. Satan thought of Dunn's Oriental cruelty.

Feverishly his fingers shuffled the papers. Seeking some s c r a p of words in American, something to reveal Dunn's present activities.

Vaguely he heard a distant booming. . . .

The papers slid under his hands on the table. His fevered grey eyes caught one with tiny microscopic writing—in English.

Too small to read.

BOOM, *boom!* Blasting somewhere?

A library should afford a reading glass. He whipped open the table drawer. A big magnifying glass lay inside on a blotter.

Studying the tiny writing under the lamp, his subconscious brain considered the unlikelihood of builders blasting foundations at two fifteen in the morning, or of battleships at target practise twenty miles out to sea.

Then all his attention became riveted on the writing. Brief curt words—memoranda. . . .

A door slammed somewhere in the house. A car started outside. But the significance of the terrible memoranda held Satan paralyzed.

An invasion! Rangoff Dunn, the local commander of civilians when the Oriental troops landed. A paralyzing blow at the vital centers on the West Coast, cutting it off from the East and Central. Complete possession from the coast to the mountains which could be h e l d against American f o r c e s coming from the Eastern and Texan military camps. A bombing expedition against San Antonio where American troops might be concentrated. And above all horrors—the ravishing of the film colonies.

American beauties in Japanese hands. The military commanders promised themselves a fine holocaust. Famous stars already bidden f o r—th e militarist Yohanshu demanded possession of a famous beauty before she was turned over to his seconds-in-command and thus it was down the line. Emperor Hirohito, it was known, had issued a military edict against the seizure or rape of white woman other than snipers, mindful of the danger of immediate interference on the part of Australia. But passion-mad orientals could hardly be controlled to that extent, especially when the opportunity for suicide was always extended an officer rather than an army court martial and the hangman's noose.

An entire Japanese half-division, equipped with lighter calibre rifles, and all speaking English, was moving in on Los Angeles from the south, west and north. The pitifully small U. S. garrison at San Francisco was doing a "Fort Sumter" and holding on in antiquated fortresses against overwhelming odds, but it was only a question of time before their masks would not be able to hold against the new gas attacks being launched at mathematically-regular intervals.

"Thank, Heaven," thought Devlin, "we didn't fall for this naval parity stuff. Maybe the Atlantic fleet can get 'round before it's too late. Got to count on ourselves, 'cause this is Europe's chance to *prove* we should have been in the League of Nations. Thank Heaven, too, for the big navy President Roosevelt started to build up!"

By some inexplicable circumstance young women from all over Hollywood and the suburbs of Los Angeles began to congregate in the great, steel-constructed studios—for mutual sympathy and possible assistance.

Long lines of aged men, cripples, "bums" from the streets and even short-term prisoners in the local, city jails just released, were forming in long lines at the studios to receive antique equipment, axes, guns, rifles of every pattern, bayonets, and swords. Heaven be praised, the home guard was forming—those whose lives meant nothing to themselves and to others. Soon they were to be swept into the awful holocaust of hell and destruction in an effort to stem the tide until troop movements from the East passed the Rockies.

Through the courtesy of the Dominion of Canada hundreds and hundreds of carloads of khaki clad soldiers were pounding the rails westward over the tracks of both the Canadian Pacific and Canadian National railroads. From the sun-warmed plantations of Georgia and Florida thousands of National Guard troops were boarding transports to sail, via the Gulf of Mexico to the Rio Grande. Southern chivalry was again out to save its white women. So it was with the Middle Atlantic States, and the New England States and the line.

War! Real war! Oriental jealousy of white beauties. Lust! Greed!

And then the tiny memorandum—that Dunn would reserve for himself one Grace Darling whom he would take from the attacked area an hour before the zero hour of March 16th.

March 16th, 1939.

The booming grew suddenly louder: the glass windows rattled.

Satan turned glazed eyes to the calender on the wall. March 15th.

But that was yesterday. His eye went to the clock. It was now two thirty on the morning of March 16th.

He stared at the memorandum through the reading glass. Zero hour—3.28, Pacific Time.

A trigger seemed to release a spring in his brain. Three leaps took him to the window. He drew aside the curtains with such force as to tear one down. Stared into a black night, spotted yellowly with street lamps in patterns below.

BOOM, *boom, boom!* The room vibrated. The whole air was vibrating to the thundrous reports. The whole atmosphere was in motion, the floor trembling under communicated concussions.

The Japs had started their attack.

Curiously he had but one thought. Darling!

That slammed door! The moving car! What else but Dunn on his way to get her, hide her away?

Oh, Satan understood now! He knew why Dunn had hated him—tried to bring him into trouble two years ago when Darling first came to Hollywood. It was not just the girl—the matter of a certain invention conceived by Satan's fertile me-

The scene within the studio was one of carnage.

chanical mind and submitted to the American War Office to be contemptuously and entirely rejected.

An invention arising out of camera-experiences . . . the effect of certain rays upon color, particularly

a destructive effect upon pale yellow, the color of the Orientals.

A scientific and amazing defense against possible aggression from Japan.

The dead-heads and brass hats had rejected the idea. They wanted wars fought according to their own red-taped rules.

Of course, Dunn being a spy. . . .

That brought him to the girl's plight. . . . Satan began running before he knew just what he was doing. Tore through the hall, flung open the front door, and sprang to the corner round which a fire-engine was screaming.

His strong hands gripped the extended ladder. It tore him off his feet. He hung on until the engine reached the street by the Mirimar

Apartments. By this time roads were crowded with panicked, half-dressed crowds. Satan hurtled his way into the apartment house, catching an elevator going to Darling's floor.

"Where's Miss Darling?" he yelled to the flustered, semi-clothed floor maid.

"I don't know, sir . . . what's all the banging outside? Is it an earthquake?"

"Her room's empty." Satan pointed to the door he had burst open and the apartment he had searched.

"Maybe she went out to see what's happening . . . is it an earthquake?" screamed the maid above the din.

"Did you see a stout man with thin lips call on Miss Darling about twenty minutes ago?" he shouted.

THE maid wrung her hands. "No —I've just wakened up. Is it an earthquake? . . ."

"No," Satan shouted as he leaped for the interior staircase. "It's WAR!"

He saw the maid fainting as he left the floor.

No use waiting for an elevator. No use hailing a taxi. He ran to the police station. Then he couldn't get a word in edgeways.

"Limousine?" barked a frazzled sergeant. "What the hell do we know—or care? Murder can be done tonight and it won't matter. We've got orders to herd the people out of the town. Start camps in the hills near water supplies. Chlorinate the drains to prevent disease."

Bang, bang! Booooooom! A great red tongue licked skyward some miles away as Satan returned to the street. War! Destruction! People were screaming a rumor: "The Japs have landed."

Satan fought his way to a parking lot, stole someone's car, and got to the Phoenix Films executive offices.

There he found his immediate superior, white-haired Sam Smiles, wry-mouthed, bleary-eyed, pyjama-ed, listening over a phone.

"Where's Miss Darling, Sam?"

"How the heck should I know? Listen to this, Satan. Pacific Fleet attacked by submarines outside San Francisco. Panama Canal locks blown up . . . we won't be able to get our Atlantic fleet across to help us now. To think I should have lived to see. . . ."

"What do you know about Dunn?" Devlin shouted in his other ear. "Hasn't he a house somewhere on the desert? A ranch or something?"

"Eh? Dunn? San Yolande ranch —sixty miles east . . . the Mayor of Los Angeles has ten minutes to surrender the city and save it from bombardment."

"They're bombarding it now, aren't they?"

"Only the railroad stations, trunk lines, main highways and bridges—"

In the outer office half-dressed executives crowded round a ticker.

Clickety-click! Click-click. Stock Exchange to be suspended!

The radio dial was being twisted by a frantic employee. It blared:

"Attention everybody! The Mayor has surrendered the city to the Japanese. People must keep to their houses. Men carrying arms will be shot . . . special to film companies. All actors and actresses must assemble at their various studios. . . ."

"What's the idea of that?" shouted

Sam from the next room. "Ridiculous, it is. . . ."

"The Jap officers mean to have their white women," grated Satan harshly as he swung from the office.

The car he had borrowed was an 80 h.p. Dusenberg. Its power helped him little on the crowded streets. Not until he passed the city limits could he really let her out. Then he glided past the hundreds of fugitives fleeing eastwards like a long, ruthless roaring shadow.

Yet so much time had been lost, that day tinted the sky when he swung the machine into the road curving to San Yolande ranch.

THE great ranch house was dark and silent. He ran round to the back with revolver drawn. No one answered his shouts. He went to the garages. Three cars there—none dusty or mud-spattered. No new tracks on the drive. He had got here before Dunn.

As he broke in the back he wondered whether Dunn had another prepared hiding place, or where on the road he had passed him. In a pantry he found edibles, fresh milk placed there the night before. This proved that Dunn meant to come here. There were Mexican servants living nearby probably. He went into the living room and almost jumped out of his skin at the raucous telephone bell behind him.

After a second he took down the receiver. Instinct made him imitate a Mexicano's accent. "Eeet is me, Senor."

"Pedro!" came Dunn's thin flinty voice over the wire. "Can you hear me?"

Satan stiffened, fingers dampening as they grasped the phone. He husked his voice: "Si, senor."

"It's me, Mr. Dunn."

"Si, senor."

"Good—the wires are m o s t l y down. . . . I want to be sure you understand me, Pedro. Your voice sounds blurred, different—can you hear me clearly?"

Satan dared risk no more than another. "Si, senor Dunn."

"My car was side-swiped by a fire engine, Pedro. I wasn't able to leave the city before they threw a cordon round it. Now I'm not allowed to leave the city, do you hear, Pedro?"

Through the window, Satan saw a sombreroed figure moving across the garden path in the early dawn. Taking the phone to the limit of its cord, he answered while he watched the real Pedro enter a chicken house with an egg basket. "Si, senor."

"So you must come to my city home and bring my black dispatch case with you, Pedro," came the tinny voice.

Satan's grey eyes dilated at the phone. "Senor?"

"Come to my house, Pedro. Listen carefully. They're allowing no one to enter or leave the city. So you must find a Japanese patrol and repeat these words to the officer: 'Samauri Dunn-y-o goes by General Fulang order. Do you hear, Pedro?"

"Si, senor."

"Then repeat the words."

Satan wet his lips and made his voice as much like a Mexican's as possible: "Samauri Dunn-y-o goes by Generala Fulanga horder."

"That's right," said Dunn after a pause. Suspicion flicked his next question: "Tell me what orders I gave you yesterday, Pedro."

It was a trap. But Satan smiled

grimly. "No can hear, Senor. Wire breako."

He heard Dunn cursing as he hung up.

The Mexican came out of the hen house. Satan threw open the window, vaulted to the lawn, and gave the Mexican a full view of a round black revolver muzzle.

"Hand over that blanket and sombrero, quick. . . ."

The frightened Mexican, denuded of most of his clothing, shivered as he showed Dunn the black dispatch case in a bedroom.

THE case was heavy, Satan took but a second to rip its locks.

Then he staggered back. A very familiar apparatus met his gaze. Gingerly he bent and touched its wires, fingered terminals, turned a switch and snapped it off as a yellow fringe of the blanket began to burn.

"Holy Moses—so that's why the War office paid no more attention to my letters. My working model was stolen from the postoffice."

The Mexican wailed: "Senor; mi sombrero—eet is cold without a blanket. . . ."

A heavy rumble of trucks came from the road some two hundred yards away. Devlin tore to the piazzo and spotted the khaki green of army lorries. His shrill whistle split the morning.

The officer on the truck he finally halted voiced angry disbelief. "I don't believe it. You're a damned crank. . . ."

"I'll give you proof," Satan snarled. He jerked the officer's arm.

The soldier drew a Colt. "None of that . . . and no tricks. We've orders to attack the Japs at the end of this road. . . ."

"Attack!" Satan laughed shortly. "Don't you realize that Los Angeles is lying under the guns of the Japanese battle fleet? The Japanese admiral has warned the mayor that one Japanese shore-going s a i l o r killed or wounded means the death of every man, woman and child in Los Angeles."

"Then you're suggesting. . . ."

"The only way to save the nation," Satan snapped as he lifted the dispatch-case lid. "This machine is only good for thirty minutes use . . . but—"

He talked rapidly for several minutes, pounding his fist.

"I'll see about it," consented the officer.

"Damn it, man: I'm calling Washington myself by phone. All you have to do is hustle this thing away. . . ."

*   *   *   *   *

It was nearing noon when an army truck set Satan down just outside the city cordon. Jap soldiers halted him with bayonets.

"Samauri Dunn-y-o goes by General Fulang's order."

"General Fulang is at headquarters in Movie Studio," said the Japanese patrol officer in broken English.

"Then take me to him," Satan snapped. "I am personal assistant to the great Japanese friend, Mr. Dunn, don't you savvy?"

"Get in side-car," ordered the Jap, striding the saddle of a motorbicycle blazoned with the Rising Sun in scarlet on the tank.

A little flag with a curious ensign breezed from the handle-bars. The Jap officer rode fast. They were not stopped until they skidded to a halt outside the big Phoenix Films main building.

"Special message for General Fulang."

"The General is in conference." Both officer and sentry grinned.

The officer got off the bike. "Come!" he said to Satan.

On the way through the downstairs corridors, Satan saw many a pretty extra being disrobed by rough, greedy yellow fingers. In the main studios many a famous star screamed and writhed under a savage, leering yellow face. But outside the executive office he heard an altercation going on inside.

The officer halted: "General Fulang is here. We go in."

He knocked at the door. Receiving no answer, timidly opened. Grinned. Became sober and saluted. "General. A special messenger from Samauri Dunn-y-o. . . ."

Satan's tall head looked over the flat top of the Jap officer's cap. His grey eyes met the narrow black slits of the famous Jap militarist. Fulang's picture had appeared on many movie news reels. In person he was deadlier than his pictures even hinted. Brilliant sparks darted from his eyes. His mouth was ruthlessness personified. A yellow claw held a girl by the shoulder.

The breath left Satan's body when he saw the girl was Darling.

Grace Darling's head was thrown back so that her yellow hair hung against the wall to which Fulang pushed her. An ugly bruise marred the satin glowing flesh of her shoulder where a nightgown had been torn away. Horror and pain curled her full red luscious mouth.

"You horrible yellow brute—let me go," she was screaming.

Then she saw Satan and her seductive eyes grew large. Her scream cut off suddenly.

"Oh!" she gasped; terrified.

Yet Satan had hardly time to glance at her then. For he was staring into the glittering eyes of the man who had been trying to separate her from General Fulang.

That man, savage, angry, amazed, was Dunn.

And Dunn was shouting at the general: "She's mine. It was arranged. Take one of the other stars. . . ."

Then Dunn, also, saw Satan and became silent through astonishment.

Only General Fulang and the officer who had admitted Satan were ignorant of the true situation.

THE officer saluted again: spoke rapidly in Japanese.

Fulang studied Satan with quick thoroughness. "You are not a Mexican. Have you not brought the bag?"

He swung on Dunn: "Did you not telephone your Mexican to bring the machine?"

Dunn reeled, stuttered: "This—isn't my Mexican. Not Pedro."

"Who is he?" snapped Fulang.

"He—he—"

"Dunn!" interrupted Satan Devlin authoritatively, and so quickly that no one but an expert linguist or an American could follow him: "Remember you're a white man. Help this girl. Tell them I'm okay."

"What does he say?" rapped the General. "Okay—what?"

Dunn's face was green. White about the gills. Clearly his quarrel with the general had upset his confidence. But he was not ready to take the daring chance Satan had held out to him. His fingers twitched.

And still as yet Fulang and his officer had no suspicion.

The agonized screams of fleeing and captured beauties were resounding through the building. Conversation had to be carried on loudly. Fulang cupped his ear: "What you say, Dunn?"

"He's an enemy!" Dunn yelled.

Simultaneously, Satan's crooked arm swept the subordinate Jap officer into a vice-like hook while his other arm shot out and choked Fulang's neck.

Fulang's cry choked to a groan. Satan's uprising foot c a u g h t Dunn's stomach.

Dunn doubled up, his shout of warning punched out of him.

"Shut the door!" Satan flung to Darling.

As she flew to obey, he crashed the Japs' heads together till they went limp in his hands.

Then he turned to Dunn. "One squeak out of you. . . ."

He felt a revolver thrust into his hand. Darling's whisper: "He's wicked. He'll trick you. . . ."

"He'll be hung when the Americans drive these yellow rats from our soil," Satan rapped out. He twirled the gun, glancing round swiftly. "Into that closet, Darling. . . ."

An opened filing cabinet had been rifled by the soldiers. He jerked out the drawers, scattering papers. Hauled the two Japs across the floor. The general, doubled up, could be crammed into the lower division. His subordinate took some tucking in. Both men's heads were cracked open. Satan closed the filing door, locked it and pocketed the key.

His gun ushered Dunn into the closet with Darling. Then Satan, too, stepped in as the room door burst open.

Through a split made previously by a bayonet, he saw three Japanese officers enter with inquiring faces.

THE Japanese jabbered. Satan caught the name Fulang.

The closet was narrow but high-ceilinged, like the room. There was ventilation. But it was a tight fit for three.

Satan tingled as he felt the whole lithe length of Darling's exquisite body charged against him with gentle, teasing pressure.

His fingers felt the exposed sections of her. There was hardly an untorn square inch of her nightie.

Evidently Dunn had whipped her out of bed in the middle of the night trying to get her to his ranch in the car, and then turning back when the cordon barred his escape.

Dunn was now on the other side of her, squashed against the closet wall, keeping silent on threat of instant death if he made a sound.

The Japs jabbered away in the room.

Satan's skin tickled to the titillating caress of a fur collar against his ear. He felt around in the darkness and realized what it was. A fur coat left by one of the secretaries in the office. Its warm sleekness was just the thing to drape Darling's nakedness. In the dark he silently lifted the fur coat off its hanger and smoothed it over her bare shoulders.

She nestled in its sleekness and pressed closer to him.

Her fragrance was in his nostrils; his hand cupped a furred breast that pounded from heartbeats beneath. His other hand held the revolver that prodded into Dunn.

Dunn's emotions might be guessed. He had seen the girl he wanted,

their bayonets. But before that shout was ended, a .44 bullet would have ripped through his body. He remained silent, hardly breathing.

"*Satan*" *entered behind t h e Orderly. A yellow claw gripped the trembling girl by the hand.*

commandeered by the Japanese general: now saved from that, he was locked up in a closet, against the seductive maiden who was arm-circled, however, by his b i t t e r enemy.

One shout—and the Jap soldiers would burst into the closet with

Satan was the calmest, perhaps. He saw the Jap officers gesticulate and then leave the room. Instantly he stepped out of the closet and rushed to the little ante-room where he knew Sam's stenographer kept canned milk and other accessories for her boss during days too busy for regular meals. He returned laden with milk, sugar, a coffee percolater with wire attached, a waxed packet of cookies, and a half-pint of brandy.

A BUGLE sounded outside. Boots clattered through the corridors. The ravishment of the studio was temporarily suspended whilst the troops lined in the square outside.

Dunn's teeth chattered. He glared evilly at Satan.

"This is an outrage," he stammered. "Do you mean to keep us locked up in this closet, all three, for ever? The Japs are sure to look in eventually and kill all of us."

"Not necessarily," s a i d Satan shortly. "They've ransacked t h e building and don't expect to find anyone or anything else."

"They'll look for General Fulang."

"Not here," said Satan, leaving the closet door ajar, yet able to be shut in a moment of danger. He found a wall plug and attached the coffee percolater. "They'll think he has gone to the Mayor or something."

"Well—well—how long will we stay here?" Dunn chattered fearfully.

"Till the Japs leave America," said Satan calmly.

"What? T-twenty years?"

"Not even twenty-days," s a i d Satan.

The same radio that had blared the bad news just twelve hours ago to the studio executives now suddenly started to whine and hum. Dunn jumped to switch it off.

"Leave it on," spanned Satan, handing Darling a cup.

The radio barked:

"Citizens of Los Angeles! All California is now in the hands of the Japanese Landing Forces. The Jap authorities wish us to broadcast their advances and victories to convince you that no resistance is possible. Abandon all hope for an American victory. A large air force has completely destroyed two troop trains dispatched from St. Louis yesterday.

"News from London, England. Simultaneously with the Japanese attack on America. British warships and troops concentrated to impose sanctions on four European nations defying the League of Nations. No hope need be expected from Great Britain until the European question is settled. Her reserves have been called to the colors to defend her own shores.

"Toronto, Canada. The Governor General has announced that Canadian troops must be sent to the help of the Mother Country. No advance will be made against Japan unless Oriental troops land on Canadian soil. The Japanese Commander-in-Chief has warned Canada against raising a volunteer army to help America. Such a move, says the Japanese, would result in immediate destruction of Canadian centers by Japanese bombing planes.

"This is Station KOX. We now join the NBC network broadcasting latest reports from New York."

"God!" said Dunn. He glared at the other two. "Know what that means? The Japs have won. They'll soon find you—find Fulang's body. Kill you, torture you . . . only I can save you. Let me go and I'll intercede for you. . . ."

"Shut up," said Satan calmly. "Attend to the coffee."

"The—the coffee!"

"You don't expect to live on air, do you?"

"But—I—I can't eat. . . ."

"Well, I can. Can you, Darling?" he smiled at the girl.

Grace Darling became conscious of a pretty white breast bobbing out of the fur coat. It lay white and satiny on the dark sparkling fur. Hastily she concealed it.

"I'm hungry as a hunter."

"We'll share the cookies then as Dunn doesn't want any."

Dunn suddenly leaped to the door.

"No, you don't." Satan's outstretched foot tripped him. Gummed paper tape from the desk soon was wound round the man's wrists and ankles, dozens of yards of it.

"Sit on him, Darling, while I take a look round," Satan half-laughed.

He grinned as the pretty girl placed her f u r r e d contours on Dunn's apoplectic visage.

The building, at least this floor of it, proved empty. He saw troops marching along the Boulevard. Some would race into houses and return with screaming young girls in all stages of undress. The yellow men were making hay.

When he returned to the room, the radio was going again:

"Detroit, Michigan. Japanese are making intensive efforts to halt the unprecedented activity taking place in several guarded factories. Planes have bombed the city but failed in three attempts to land troops. . . ."

The announcer's voice s t o p p e d abruptly.

"They've shut him off the air for saying something unfavorable to Japanese morale," commented Satan admiring the way that Darling's s h a p e l y calves were crossed on Dunn's perspiring face. Certainly she proved a very lovely jailer.

"Will anyone bother us here?" she giggled with the rebounding spirits of youth.

"I don't think so," Satan surmized. "The Japs can't spare troops enough to patrol every building in Hollywood and Los Angeles. All we have to do is stay here until. . . ."

"Until?" she whispered anxiously.

He shrugged: *"Quin sabe?"*

"Where shall we sleep?" she queried suddenly.

"We'd better stick to the closet."

"All three of us?" she broke into a snigger.

"Why not?"

"There won't be room for him?" She dug a heel into Dunn.

Satan eyed the man's stoutness. "Oh, Dunn will come in handy as a mattress for us both."

"L OOK!" gasped Darling at the window on the third day.

Satan glanced over the sill. Rolling smoke hid the horizon.

"They're burning the city," she cried. "I wonder what's happening?"

"Something big," he mused. "The radio's been dead since yesterday. That means the Jap's haven't any more victories to report."

"But if they burn the city . . . no fire engines to put out the fires . . . we'll all be burned to death."

"We couldn't stay here any longer anyway," he pointed out. "No more food left . . . and the water supply stopped at noon. It may never come on again."

A groan came from the closet. "Don't leave me here to burn."

Satan glanced across at the purple-faced, bleary-eyed Dunn. Three nights as a mattress had not improved him. They must have been very trying nights for the traitor.

A human mattress might n o t mind being used by a dainty, shapely soft maiden in a fur coat, but an addition of two hundred pounds of pure bone and muscle with sharp angles was another matter.

Satan had moved out the filing cabinet containing Fulang's body and the officer's corpse on the first night. He had tried to fit himself once into their uniforms, but the difference in size was too great.

S O THEY would have to try their escape in their own clothes.

He watched the rolling clouds of smoke, purple, reddish, and black.

"I wonder. . . ."

"Wonder what?" breathed Darling.

He jumped to his feet and fiddled with the radio. "There must be some other stations broadcasting. If only we could get New York direct—or an English station on the short waves."

"I wonder the Japs haven't cut off the current."

"Their staff will need it, you see. Of course, if t h e y burn the city. . . ." He spun the d i a l s quickly; then slowly.

"Nothing on the American. Maybe the United States Government has shut down on broadcasting to preserve some s e c r e t movements. Ah. . . ." He put his ear to the screen.

"What is it?" Darling clung to him.

"A voice . . . wait, steady . . . station call. . . ."

"New York?"

"No: it's an X something. That means a Mexican station. X-E-M-A . . . that's Tampico. Listen. . . ."

The voice became audible in the room. "These Am-aireecan factories, so queek, have made by mass production. . . ." The voice faded.

Darling's little fingers twisted in Satan's "What was he saying?"

"Damn—if only I—" he muttered, manipulating the dials.

Suddenly a voice leaped from the radio.

"Victories—smashing defeat—fifty thousand wiped out. . . ."

The voice stopped.

"Who? Who won?" Darling cried frenziedly.

"I'll get that station again," he swore. "Here—"

The voice rose again, excitedly: "Complete destruction. T h e machines manufactured s e c r e t l y by bringing all the technical forces of American industry into line and skilled co-operation, armed three regiments of infantry and one artillery unit within four days. Never in the history of civilization has so supreme an instance of organization t u r n e d a ghastly defeat into a smashing t r i u m p h for civilization. . . ."

"Look out!" the girl screamed, twisting round.

Satan started, pitched forward against the radio. The radio crashed to the floor, ending t h e news. Sparks shot through Satan's head. He groped blindly along the wall, trying to keep balance. The instrument that had stunned him, struck the back of his neck. All went black. He felt himself falling. His hand caught a wire. He tugged it. The wire, tightening from the fallen radio to the wall plug, rose and tripped Dunn at the instant of striking a third time.

Dunn tripped over the wire at the instant he grabbed the girl. Satan opened dizzy eyes to see a swimming room . . . vaguely he picked out the bigger image and leveled his revolver. It leaped in his hand. Its bullet, smashing through the traitor's chest, staggered him as he rose. Dunn rolled on his back, choking, then motionless.

"Are you hurt bad?" Darling dropped by Satan's side.

He lifted himself on an elbow. "Am I dreaming, punch drunk? Listen? Do I hear. . . ."

"What—t h a t s o u n d—outside? Whistles?"

"Fifes!" he panted. "To the window. . . ."

They craned out. Down the Boulevard came swinging khaki figures. And each figure but those of the front unit carried curiously shaped machines.

"What are they?" Darling gasped.

"My invention," Satan shouted. "I gave the model to an officer to rush by plane to Washington. Can you beat it? That's what the Detroit factories made by the thousand. The ray that destroys yellow men. . . . Listen. . . ."

To the shrill strains of "Yankee Doodle Went to Town," he swung her in his arms. "Now you'll enter pictures with all honor," he gloated. "The girl who helped the man who helped drive the Japs into the Pacific. But I think I'll ask you to take all the publicity."

She glanced sideways and down, swiftly, mischief shading her eyes. "And Dunn? . . ."

"We won't mention him. That mattress episode mustn't be understood by the reformers," he chuckled devilishly.

"G-Man" Hoover Likes Movies

WE have always claimed that the movies aid the war against the criminal; and never encourage it, and no less a person that the "big chief" of the G-Men himself "goes to bat" on the subject. In Washington, D. C., recently, headquarters of the Department of Justice as well as the home of the House of Representatives, definite action was taken. Meeting the attack on so-called gangster pictures, C. C. Pettijohn read into the record at the House hearing on block booking a letter to him from J. Edgar Hoover, chief of the Federal Bureau of Investigation, as non-partisan testimony.

"At the beginning of this cycle of films," the chief "G-man" wrote, "there were several that I thought could be improved upon from the viewpoint of the enforcement officer. I promptly took up my thoughts on that subject with the organized industry heads and I received their most prompt and splendid cooperation. You are, of course, familiar with those facts because it was largely through you that these very fine results were obtained.

"In my opinion, motion pictures were a most important factor in bringing home to the American people the facts that: (a) crime is an organized business; (b) a gangster is a rodent that must be eliminated from American life; (c) respect and cooperation of the public with law enforcement officers was materially advanced."

Retake for

By FRANK E. MARKS

"WELL, here's s o m e - t h i n g," Opal Talmage said enthusiastically as her eyes riveted on the newspaper under her arms. She t u r n e d to Gordon Joslyn who dragged on a cigarette and was stretched out lazily on a davenport in her room. It was a hot Sunday afternoon in Pleasantville and Opal was dressed, or rather undressed, for comfort.

Joslyn looked possessively at the golden-haired girl, prone on the rug. His eyes sparkled, for Opal was a delectable feminine morsel to possess. Right now her only garment was a sheer black robe of cobwebby silk which by contrast made the expanse of milky white flesh beneath all the more thrilling. Her arched back was a graceful curve beginning at her rounded shoulders, dipping slightly at the waist, rising again and then m e l t i n g into tapering thighs, bare, glowing below the bunched-up robe. As Opal spoke and rolled on her side, the silken folds at her throat fell open and a firm full mound, claret-tipped and with tiny purple veins meandering through the snowy flesh popped from its filmy concealment.

Joslyn's eyes devoured the audacious ravishing hillock. "You're s o m e t h i n g, honey!" he replied. "What are you reading about?"

"About a chance to get into moving pictures—go to Hollywood!"

"Moving pictures? What does it say in the rag?"

"Don't you know what's in your own newspaper—you—ace reporter of the *Courier?*"

"I don't write the ads," Gordon Joslyn replied, got up and squatted on the floor beside Opal. He put his arm around her cuddly shoulders and looked at the newspaper on the rug. It announced a contest con-

One by one the con-testants were elim-inated until only three remained.

A romantic story of the poor little country girl who "made good" out in Hollywood

ROMANCE

ducted by the paper in co-operation with a Hollywood producing company.

"Do you think I'd have a chance w i t h that red-haired charmer, Eunice Crawford, in the running? She'll enter sure enough."

Joslyn flushed a little. His mouth clamped against her moist crimson lips and his hand captured a pliant firm melon that oozed deliciously between his fingers and made his nerves tingle. "You've got Eunice skinned in all the places, honey!"

"Did you find that out last night when you took her to the dance?"

Gordon Joslyn flushed again. "I took her because you wouldn't go."

"I had to work. But skip it!" Opal's attention returned to the feature article in the *Pleasantville Courier*. Her eyes grew wistful, dreamy. "Imagine—a trip to Hollywood and a contract to play a part in a movie!"

"Yeah, and imagine me as your husband, Mr. Opal Talmage. Nuts!"

Opal ran her pointed little tongue over Joslyn's lips. "Jealous!" she taunted. "When I become a movie queen you can be my manager. Now get out your pad and pencil and write a nice big page-one article. All about Miss Opal Talmage signing up to win the big beauty competition."

"You're gorgeous, honey!" Joslyn breathed. He gathered her up bodily in his arms and held her closely to himself. Opal felt her bare flesh against him and her breasts mashed to his chest. He laid her down among the pillows of the davenport and crowded against her warm leg. His mouth was again on her humid lips, hard, forcing them apart.

Her fiery tongue darted, contacting his, making electrifying delightful shivers scamper to every nerve in her body. His lips lowered, to the hollow of her throat. Then his palm closed over one of those firm thrusting mounds and she winced ecstatically as its flinty nodule was pressed between his fingers.

With both her own hands Opal held Joslyn tighter to her throbbing breast. She eased her golden-haired head d e e p e r into the cushion, dropped her long velvety lashes and breathed audibly, gaspingly. And then her blood tingled and bounded as she felt the brushing caress of his fingers. She circled his head, drew him down. "Gordon! Love me!"

GAY decorations festooned the main street of Pleasantville. A band played. People jostled for points of vantage near the platform in the civic center where ten of Pleasant County's fairest daughters were to be judged for grace and charm and pulchritude.

Opal Talmadge was fourth in line. Her feminine c o n t o u r s swelled smoothing, every curve a symphony beneath the sheen of her purple one-piece bathing suit. Her hair rippled in golden ringlets, her violet eyes smiling first at the judges and then at the crowd. Opal whispered to the girl alongside of her, Eunice Crawford, the flame-haired siren whom Gordon Joslyn had taken to the dance the previous week. "My legs are trembling!"

"Hold them steady, kid," Eunice replied out of the corner of her mouth. "You need *legs*, plenty, in Hollywood!"

Opal gathered her nerves and smiled at Gordon Joslyn behind the judges' chairs. Applause greeted each contesting girl who undulated to the center of the stand. The five judges made futile little marks on pieces of paper and looked bewildered. One of them approached the ten contestants and spoke in a low tone. "I—I think you girls had better retire behind the platform for a few moments while we ballot."

Opal and the other girls stepped down from the platform. She listened. The man who had spoken to them was saying, "Our task has been difficult, folks. We h a v e reached only a semi-decision. Of all the competitors, three are outstanding. So we are going to leave the final choice to you, the public. The winner will be the one who receives the greatest volume of applause."

Underneath the stage Opal's pulse raced. Would she be one of the three. A boy appeared, grinning. He had a slip of paper in his hand. "Number Two, Number S e v e n and—" Opal's heart s e e m e d to stop!— "Number Nine, are wanted back on top."

Opal caught her breath. She was Number Nine!

She turned to the other two girls who had been called. Number Two w a s a p e t i t e brunette from a neighboring town; Seven was the red-haired charmer, Eunice Crawford. Nervously the three girls returned to the stand. A thunderous wave of applause greeted them.

A judge raised the hand of the little brunette. Like a sudden pattering shower, the handclaps came. He lifted Opal's hand. The applause grew in vigor. He moved to the side of Eunice Crawford. The handclapping remained constant in volume. The little brunette smiled resignedly and left the platform. The judge shook his head. "We can't

have two q u e e n s—two winners. Let's try again." Eunice's hand was elevated. The applause was terrific. He moved to Opal. The response seemed equally strong. Back to Eunice. Deafening roar. Opal again. Were the cheers a shade louder, more emphatic? The judge cupped his ear. Somebody whistled—and the roar trebled.

No question about it now! Opal was one charming blush as she realized that she had won!

THEN came the day of Opal's departure, the bustle at the railroad station and the farewells. Gordon Joslyn was the last to leave her compartment in the coach. "I'm going to miss you, baby, when you're in Hollywood."

"I'll write often, Gordon. And . . . I won't forget you."

"You'd better not. I'm going to see that you get lots of publicity in the *Courier*." His mouth clamped lingeringly on her lips, his hand crept up her side, under her armpit and pressed a throbbing breast.

Opal's n e r v e s tingled. Gordon Joslyn was her first love. It was hard to leave him. "Good-bye, Gordon," she said fondly.

"Good-bye, darling. I'll be out in Hollywood before you know it." And with that he was gone.

Then the California Flier moved out of the depot, and Pleasantville —and Gordon—faded into the distance. Opal Talmage, future moviestar, was westward bound. . . .

* * * * *

The very first day in Hollywood was disappointing to Opal Talmage. The studio to which she reported was located on Poverty Row —that ramshackle street of buildings where 'quickies'—cheap unpretentious productions, were turned out with a rapidity matched only by the producers' lack of adequate finances.

But as the days went on Opal became more contented. After all she was working, acting before a camera whose magic eye would reproduce her talking moving self and the folks back in Pleasantville would lean forward to see their o w n b e a u t y queen scintillating before them on the screen of the local theatre.

COACHED and tutored at every turn by the director, Cliff Harding, Opal wore evening gowns of rustling silk that fit her form like poured water and whose daringly-slashed front unhampered her full white breasts that bounced gelatinously as she walked over the rugs of the drawing room set. Opal soon forgot that she was on Poverty Row.

And then arrived the morning when Opal found herself on location. The troupe was on San Clemente Island, sixty miles off the California coast. It was an uninhabited mountainous isle w h e r e curious spectators would not interfere. Opal was in her canvas dressing room, clad solely in sheer stepins and standing before the mirror. She dusted her body with talc until her flesh was like glowing marble. Her flawless skin needed no greasepaint base and she lined her full lips with crimson, kohled her eyes and punched her red nails through her golden hair. Opal g l a n c e d through the opening of the tent flap; at the swells of the Pacific that rolled, turned and hissed on the glistening sands of the beach.

The cameraman s t o o d by his blimp—the sound-proof metal case enclosing the camera. His assistant connected up the film reels. Men were placing white screens to reflect the light into the fronds of the cocoanut trees planted on the shore. Technicians arranged dangling microphones on the swinging metal arms. Opal thrilled. It was glorious!

And then as she looked her mouth dropped open. There was a chatter of laughing feminine voices. Opal stared in amazement. Running, pirouting, tripping over the sand came at least thirty tawny-skinned native girls onto the set.

And every one of the gorgeously-modeled girls was stark naked!

Opal Talmage watched with widened eyes. The girls' bodies were like smoky animated velvet. They had hair like anthracite. The thighs of every one of them were smooth columns of tawny texture. Their b r e a s t s were full, nubile, pear-shaped and jiggled provocatively, enticingly as they fringed the water's edge, dropped onto the beach; draped themselves on the sand.

Opal gasped as she saw the assistant director giving them instructions and the cameraman sighting his finder. W e r e those tawny-skinned native girls to be photographed like that—completely unclothed? Where could such moving pictures ever be shown? No U.S. censorship board w o u l d sanction such film!

So intent was Opal staring at the scene that she didn't hear; didn't notice the lifting of the tent-flap behind her. A voice said, "The native girls await their white queen! In other words, Miss Talmadge, we're ready to shoot." Opal whirled and stared into the face of the director, Cliff Harding.

Her whole body flushed. She raised her hands, tried to hide her swelling breasts. "Oh!" she caught her breath. She trembled under the scrutinizing stare of Harding who was taking in every feminine charm of her classic body.

"Just about ready?" the director asked.

"Wh-why I haven't seen my costume yet!"

Cliff Harding grinned. "Here it is." He picked up an article from a chair back. "I left it here before you came in."

Opal gasped and stared at his extended hand. *He held a mere zephyr of a G-string and bandeau!*

"You—you mean I'm going to be in front of the camera with—with only that on?"

Cliff Harding nodded. "It's more than the other girls are wearing—at that!" He motioned toward the bevy of tawny-skinned girls cavorting on the beach.

Opal's flesh burned. To go out there in the bright sunlight, in view of all those men, be photographed wearing next to nothing! She had seen no script of the picture story; had worked from day to day by oral instructions. No wonder they had come to this deserted island to shoot the scene. "But—but I can't go out there this—this way! What kind of a picture is it?"

"Don't you know?" Cliff Harding asked. "The title of the story is, THE PALE QUEEN. That's you— the star! This scene is a South Sea Island sequence. Out on the beach are your native subjects."

"But—but they can never exhibit such—such a picture!"

"Not in this country, my dear. But in South America it's different. The Argentines allow the stuff. So

I'm directing, THE PALE QUEEN. I needed a job."

It occurred to Opal that she, too, needed a job. Almost her last dollar had gone to pay the rent of a swanky apartment on Gower Street in Hollywood. There had been many dollars more in her mind's eye. But this picture would never be seen by other producers; would not gain her publicity.

SHE felt as if she would like to run from the tent. Refuse to go out there almost stark naked before that camera. Quit!

But there were sixty miles of ocean between her and San Pedro, and only the company's chartered tug to take her back. There was helplessness on her features as she lifted her velvety lashes to Cliff Harding.

He patted her rounded shoulder. "Come on, you'll get used to it." Harding pressed her closer and she melted to him. There was something soothing about the feel of his arms, some vague sense of protection.

"All—all right," Opal said. "I'll do it!"

"Good girl! Hurry out." Harding left the tent.

Opal looked at her glowing body in the mirror—bare white flesh for greedy eyes in another continent. She adjusted the frail garment and gasped. She might as well be stark naked—like those native girls!

Throwing a robe around herself, Opal left the tent and went to where Cliff Harding stood beside the camera. The director outlined the scene; gave her instructions. Everything was in readiness. With trembling fingers Opal dropped her robe.

Even the tawny-skinned g i r l s

g a s p e d at Opal's loveliness; so white, so gorgeous, gleaming in the sun. "Grand!" she heard Director Harding praise and saw his eyes rest on the sweeping curves of her satiny body and her vibrant columnar thighs.

Then for the next hour Opal flitted in the sea spray, raised her arms as if in supplication to the world. She had close-ups when it seemed that the rigid centers of her bosoms almost touched the camera lens. There was a scene where the tawny maidens surrounded Opal, their queen, peerless among them. The native girls dropped to their knees, bent forward, breasts dipping.

Opal suddenly screamed. The native girls fled. Bounding upon her was a bronzed giant. He bowled Opal to the sand. He looked down into her upturned face as if he were her conqueror. His hands laved her breasts, her thighs and legs. He lifted her above his head, strode toward the camera and the dangling microphone overhead. With Opal over his shoulder he ran down the beach as if he had captured a slave. Then he stopped, dumped her down, grinned and started back to the set. It had been a scene—a scene too real for Opal. . . .

FOR nine days more Opal worked in costume at the ramshackle studio on Poverty row. She had almost forgotten about the risque shots on the island. Then, on the tenth day, Cliff Harding handed her a check. "It's all over—the picture's ready for cutting."

Opal's violet eyes widened. "You—you mean there's no more work for me?"

"Nor for any of us. I finished the thing on schedule. Got any plans?"

Dazed, Opal shook her head. "I—I thought I was to work for this company permanently." A lump choked her throat.

Harding smiled. "There's no permanence on this type of picture, my dear. I've got a chance to do an opus for Jake Wolf later on. Maybe I could get you a bit."

"Oh, I hope so, soon," she said earnestly.

Cliff Harding came closer. There seemed to be compassion in his eyes. "How about taking a ride with me to the beach tonight? We'll have dinner."

"Good. I'll call for you at seven. Be ready?"

Opal nodded happily. . . .

That night Opal wore her laciest frock. Harding honked for her five minutes ahead of time. She hurried out and nestled beside him in the cushions of the low-hung, sporty roadster. They swung off along a wide boulevard.

"Where are we going?" Opal wanted to know.

"Malibu," Harding answered.

"Where all the stars have beach houses?"

Harding smiled. "Directors have beach houses, too."

Malibu, playground of the stars. Opal thrilled to the salt tang of the air as they came to the little Pacific colony. Harding stopped before a tiny surf-side cottage. "Here's my place." He helped her from the car, along the walk and into the cottage. A table was laid for two. Harding shook up a cocktail.

After eating, Opal sat some distance from where Harding lolled on the davenport. He reached down for a tissue-wrapped box. "I have something for you, dear," he said.

Opal sat beside him as he opened the package. "It's a negligee!" she exclaimed and fingered the sheer diaphanous garment.

"The girl in the important role for Jake Wolf's picture will wear something like this; thought you might be interested in a little private dress rehearsal."

Opal's nerves tensed. He wanted her to wear this intimate lacy gown here in this cottage, alone for a try-out with him! She hesitated, licked her dry lips. But what did it matter? After all he had seen her, sans apparel on San Clemente Island. She took the lacy raiment and went into the next room. After a few moments she reappeared.

Cliff Harding sprang to his feet. His eyes sparkled as he downed a straight whiskey. Opal felt his glance sweep her form, so visible through the sheer silken fabric, come to rest on the protruding hillocks of her breasts, lower to her gleaming thighs, scarce covered by the diaphanous negligee. She felt more confused than on the island where she had company in her nakedness. "You're gorgeous!" Harding breathed.

HE pulled her down on the davenport close beside himself. His arm stole over her shoulder, drawing her near, his hand touched on a resilient mound. Opal felt the apex go flinty and a sudden tremor scurried over her. He eased her back and his head lowered, his lips meeting her.

Opal panted and little tingles darted through her nerves. Her blood began to pound as his hand touched the warm flesh of her thigh. She felt flaming from his caresses.

For the next hour they took some of the most daring close-ups Opal had ever known.

Not since she had been in Gordon Joslyn's arms back in Pleasantville had she felt such desires overpowering her. But that was different. Gordon was her first love—was going to marry her some day—had a right to her!

Abruptly Opal sprang from Cliff Harding's arms. "No, please!" she panted. "I can't! I want to go home!"

Harding shrugged. "Okay, baby." He got up. "I'll take you home. . . ."

OPAL saw no more of Cliff Harding, the director, after that night. Her days were spent in a weary round of the studios. It was the same answer from every casting director, "No work today." Time went on. Her funds shrank. She wrote cheerful letters to Gordon Joslyn, reporter back home on the Pleasantville *Courier*. Never would she let him or the folks back there know the truth—that she had been a failure.

And then came a letter from Gordon that threw her into a paroxysm of humiliation and fear. "I'll be in Hollywood soon," Gordon wrote.

She must keep him from Hollywood at any cost; prevent him from discovering that her letters saying she was a success were monstrous lies. There was but one sure way. She wrote to him.

"Dear Gordon," she penned and fought desperately to dam the tears. "I may as well tell you. There is no need for you to come to Hollywood. You're a small-town boy. I've gone Hollywood. I've had to make—well, sacrifices for my career. Directors don't give girls work without—payment. Better if we never saw one another again. Good-bye. Opal."

After mailing the letter the following morning Opal made the round of the studios again. On the lot of Imperial Productions she ran into the manager of the studio restaurant. "Looking for a job, girlie?" he grinned.

Opal whirled, pulse racing. "Here—for Imperial?"

The man nodded. "Sure. I need a waitress."

Opal's face reddened. "I'm an actress!"

"I know it, girlie; never hire anything else but."

Opal smiled wryly as she thought of Pleasantville. What would the band which had serenaded at the depot have played if they had known that she was going to Hollywood to wait tables? Suddenly her chin went up. A job was a job. "Okay," she said to the man. "I'll work for you."

Then a month of rushing quick lunches. A month during which she had the crowning humiliation of serving Cliff Harding, her former director—Harding who showed up one day at the lunch room, nodded and greeted her casually, "Hello, little one, getting experience?"

Opal flushed. "I'm earning a living," she retorted. Then curiously, "Are you working here?"

The director nodded. "Got a contract to do ten pictures for Imperial—started this morning. Bring me a chicken salad."

A week later, Opal, arrestingly-pert in her waitress uniform, came through the service door of the kitchen restaurant. Abruptly she stopped and drew a sharp breath. Seated alone at the counter was Gordon Joslyn, her sweetheart from back home in Pleasantville!

Joslyn hadn't seen her—mustn't

see her! Not after that damning letter about herself and the lies she had written about her cinema success. Panicky she ran back in the kitchen and set down her tray. A plan struck her. She grabbed her handbag, delved for her cosmetics. She applied rouge and powder and lipstick and kohl with a lavish touch.

Opal went back into the lunch room. She spoke guardedly to another waitress. For a moment she felt as if she wanted to rush into Gordon's arms, confess her lies, implore his forgiveness. But she couldn't do that now. Better to still let him believe that she had gone Hollywood. She slipped up on the stool alongside him and spoke with feigned surprise, "Gordon! Of all persons! How's everything back in the corn belt?"

Gordon Joslyn t u r n e d startled eyes. "Opal! You! Are you working here on the Imperial lot?" He scanned her waitress uniform.

"Yes, Gordon. But I do look like the other waitresses in this joint, don't I? I'm in costume for a picture—a restaurant scene." Opal turned to the waitress behind the counter. "Clara, slip me doughnuts and coffee! I'm in a rush."

"Yes, Miss Talmage," the girl replied.

Opal talked fast. "Well, Gordon, how's Eunice, the red-haired devil who gave me such a close shave in the beauty contest?"

Gordon Joslyn reddened a bit. "She—she's fine."

Opal gulped her coffee while she fought back a lump in her throat. "Must race back to the set, Gordon; director's waiting."

He grasped her hand. "But I'm going to see you act. . . ." He looked at his watch. "I'm to meet a chap here who came out with me. We're attending a convention. I'll be through with him soon. What set are you working on?"

Opal scarcely heard his last question. Then Gordon hadn't come to Hollywood just to see her. What rotten luck that he had stumbled upon her in a restaurant.

"What set are you on?" Joslyn asked again.

Opal went icy. All her fabrications about herself in pictures were about to be discovered. Without thought she answered, "I'm working for Cliff Harding. He's a director for Imperial. Ask anyone— they'll direct you to his stage." Face flaming, she dashed out of the lunch-room.

OUTSIDE, the significance of her lie made her tremble. But she must send Gordon back to Pleasantville believing that she was a success. But Gordon was going to visit the set. She thought of Cliff Harding. Could he help her? What would be his price? She remembered that night in the Malibu cottage.

Instinctively she hurried to the Imperial administration building. Abruptly she came face to face with Harding himself. She blanched. "I—I'm in s e r i o u s trouble!" she blurted.

Cliff Harding raised his brows. "Can I help?"

"You're the only one who can!"

He piloted her into the studio. "Tell me about it."

"It's—it's a friend from my home town. He's here—he's coming in to watch me act!"

Cliff Harding smiled. "Act?"

Opal nodded, flushing. "I—I lied to him. I've been writing back home, boasting of my success in pictures. He saw me in this waitress uniform. I told him I was in costume; working in the picture you're directing. Oh, Mr. Harding—Cliff—you must help me! I—I'll do anything if—if you'll help me!"

Harding surveyed her with an inscrutable twinkle in his eye. "You'd do anything?"

OPAL dropped her lashes. She realized what he meant. But she was committed too far to her plan to r e t r e a t now. Flushing, she nodded.

"Is your—er, friend, coming right away?" She nodded again, distrait.

Cliff Harding grinned. "Okay. I'll help you slip it over. Come on. I'll get the property boy to set up three or four tables. It'll look enough like a cafe to pass muster." He turned to the doorman. "If anybody wants to know where I'm shooting, send them to stage 5."

Inside the great studio proper, Harding led her toward a sound-proofed stage. Carefully they picked their way over coils of wire, discarded props, painted scenes, banks of lights, ducking under hanging microphones here and there. Harding looked at Opal. "Better fix your make-up. I'll round up a couple of electricians, a sound mixer and a cameraman. I'll borrow a few extras for atmosphere. Be back in a minute." He disappeared.

Opal freshened her make-up with hands that trembled with excitement. The cinema virus was in her blood; and even though she knew the coming scene was to be a pure fake, she thrilled at the idea of being once more in front of a camera, once more speaking lines that would be recorded.

Harding returned, in his wake a motley crowd. There were several extras—men and women whose yellow-painted faces and saffron-tinted shirts and dresses would appear snowy white in the completed film. The director seated them at tables. Under his guidance a camera was trained on the scene. An electrician snapped various lights on and off. A "mixer"—the man in charge of the microphone and recording apparatus—swung his pick-up instrument high over the set. He turned a switch on his mixing panel and applied the earphones to his head; listening intently.

Suddenly Opal went cold all over. "He's—he's coming in!" she whispered to Cliff Harding.

"Your friend from back home?"

"Yes. Can't we get started?"

Harding smiled. "Don't you want to talk with him first?"

"No! I don't want to talk to him now or later!"

"It's your party. Okay, let's go!" Harding said in a raised voice. The banked lights flashed into brilliance. Cliff Harding assumed his best directorial manner. "You e x t r a s— you're dining in a restaurant. Miss Talmage, you enter from offstage right, carrying a tray. Serve the people at the nearest table. Then go to the next table and take their orders. As you pass the third table, the man there will stop you and say, 'Where is my steak?' Then you answer 'I'll bring it right in, sir.' Got it?"

O p a l and the extras nodded. Harding turned to the grip-boy. The youngster chalked a hieroglyph on a slate and stepped in front of the camera.

"Quiet, everybody!" H a r d i n g called. Silence descended. C l i f f

Harding nodded and yelled, "Interlock!"

The c a m e r a whirled silently. Then the grip-boy lowered the slate and spoke in a loud voice. "Harding, scene seven, take two," he intoned into the dangling microphone. He raised a peculiar-looking rod that had a hemispherical wooden block at either end. The boy clicked a trigger. The upper block descended along the rod and clicked against the lower piece of wood. The scene was under way.

Opal carried out her part like a veteran. Just as she finished the delivery of her lines, Harding called a sudden halt, and turned in his tracks. The director faced Gordon Joslyn, who had approached and stood behind the camera, watching with avid interest. Harding scowled. "Beat it—I don't allow visitors on my stage!"

Gordon Joslyn turned brick-red and held forth a studio pass. "But —credentials. I'm a regular newspaper man!" he asserted.

"Don't give a damn! I don't allow sight-seers. Scram!"

"But—I want to talk to Miss Talmage—" Joslyn sputtered.

"She's busy, working! See her after studio hours. Get out!" Gordon Joslyn, flushed and angry, turned and left.

Cliff Harding grinned at Opal, and waved dismissal to the other persons on the set. "Well, I put it over for you, didn't I? I even got rid of your boy friend, as you seemed to desire."

"How—how can I ever thank you?" Opal faltered.

"Well, you might invite me up to visit you this evening. Then maybe I'll let you pour out your most profuse gratitude." His eyes were twinkling again.

"If—if you like," Opal replied.

"I'll be there with bells on!"

THE clock on the mantel in the living room of Opal Talmage's flat tinkled eight times. The buzzer announced a caller. Opal opened the door. Cliff Harding smiled as she bade him enter. "You were grand in that scene today, little one," he told her.

"And you'll never know how big a favor you did for me today," Opal replied sincerely. She eyed him curiously. "You're quite prompt in collecting your debts, aren't you?"

He grinned. "What a splendid opinion you have of me!"

"Rather, I have a good memory."

Harding looked uncomfortable. "You don't regret that Malibu incident half as much as I do, Opal!"

Opal started to answer. Her words were interrputed by the raucous ringing of the telephone. She picked up the receiver—and then she went suddenly pale. Gordon Joslyn's voice, unfamiliarly thick, floated over the wire. "I'm down in the lobby, baby—coming right up!" There was a click as Joslyn disconnected.

Opal turned frightened eyes to Cliff Harding. "It—it's Gordon Joslyn—the boy from my home town! He's coming up here!"

Harding's brows rose sarcastically. "Unexpectedly—or is this your scheme for evading the wicked villain?"

"N—no! I didn't know he was coming—never gave him my address even. Won't you please keep out of sight while he's here?"

Harding smiled. "Anything to oblige so charming a hostess." He moved into the little kitchenette, closing the door.

The doorbell buzzed. Opal answered it—to behold a Gordon Joslyn she had never seen before. His hair was rumpled, his eyes bleary. As he walked into the apartment he swayed. "Found your address in the phone directory," he explained thickly. He stared in a fashion that frightened her. It was as though he were a savage beast, ready to tear the clothes from her body. "Got a little kiss for your old playmate?"

Opal backed away. "Gordon! You're drunk!"

"Yeah—this Los Angeles gin's got lots of authority. As long as I was out here I decided to go Hollywood —like you did!" He made a flying grab for her.

Opal side-stepped away. "What do you think I am?"

"I think you're exactly what you said you were in your last letter to me—a common little—"

Her hand was over his mouth. "Listen Gordon. I've lied to you in my letters! I told you I was a success in pictures. I wasn't. I was a rotten failure. I was working as a waitress. It was the only job I could get. You wrote about coming out to see me. I didn't want you to come—didn't want you to find out what a washout I'd turned out to be! So I wrote you a lie. I told you I'd become—well, what you just started to call me. But it was a lie, Gordon! I swear it was a lie!"

Joslyn backed off and clapped his hands drunkenly. "Some scene, kid —you're a swell actress! But you're not pulling anything over on little Gordon. Now—are you going to kiss me, or shall I take it away?"

OPAL muffled an involuntary scream as Gordon Joslyn dived for her. His hand snatched at the throat of her light summer gown. There was a ripping as Joslyn in his drunken frenzy jerked. Opal backed away as her wrecked gown fell in tatters around her feet. She crouched, shrank to the wall, her flushed body clothed only in lacy step-ins, her breasts heaving.

The kitchenette door banged open. Cliff Harding leaped into the room, his face a thunder-cloud. Joslyn whirled and spied the director. "Oh, now I get it!" he grunted. "That's why you wouldn't c o m e across, baby; had another lover in hiding. I butted in on your party." He faced the director. "Your night, fella! My turn tomorrow night!"

Cliff Harding's fist shot out. It caught Joslyn on the jaw. Joslyn went down, dazed. He struggled to his feet, swayed. Harding spoke, "Get out—don't come back tomorrow night or any other night!"

"Steady customer, eh?" Joslyn snarled. "Okay. *I'm damned glad my wife didn't win that beauty con-*

test!" Opal gasped, "Your—your wife, Gordon?"

Gordon Joslyn g r i n n e d mockingly. "Yeah, married Eunice Crawford the month after you left. I let you keep on writing to me—wanted copy for the *Courier.* Well, I'll be seein' you. And when I get back to Pleasantville, I'll send you a copy of the paper. You know—all about Opal Talmage—Pleasantville's movie queen. Maybe you think I won't tell all the boys and girls just what kind of a Holywood success their little Opal turned out to be!"

Joslyn reached the door when Cliff Harding's voice halted him. "Just a minute! I'm warning you, if you print a word of what you suggest, your paper will have the biggest libel suit they ever heard of! Because—Miss Talmage is actually going to be featured in Imperial Productions! Her tests today turned out so well that I came here tonight especially to offer her a contract. Now—get out. And stay out!"

As the door slammed behind Joslyn, Opal turned to the director. "Mr. Harding—Cliff—do—you—"

The twinkle was returning to his eyes. "I really mean that you're going to be cast in my next picture." And then his strong arms were around her and she felt her warm body against him. His mouth was on her wet lips. "You're going to be my leading lady—off the screen as well as on!"

Impulsively Opal clung to him. "Cliff—do you still have that cozy little cottage at Malibu?"

"I'll never give that up, darling."

"Cliff," she breathed. "Take me down there, tonight, now. It's nice there. I want to hear the sea. I want to wear that silken negligee, with you, alone, Cliff!!!"

MARCIA of the MOVIES

Jack Spender, G-Man By Eric Brosker

The Wasp

Clipped for a thousand dollars by a Hollywood siren—but it couldn't buy real love!

By JULIE HOWE

SOMETIMES, in the opinion of this story teller, there are things worse than the sacrifice of virtue or honor—or am I wrong? The paths of virtue lead but to the grave, they say in Hollywood, when they speak of those who live in the pictures. The first stumbling block in the path to stardom is a girl's own innocence, they explain; and those baser in mind claim that an actress must be "ruined" to be made.

Oh, there are butterflies who scorch their wings, of course; plenty of them; little gaudy butterflies lured by the light of fame or money. But there are always more, and who but themselves directed their flight into the flame?

There are hundreds of butterflies coming to Hollywood every day—but Madelynn Hope was a wasp, a wise little wasp who knew the danger of fire and skilfully avoided it.

She had nothing but scorn for the butterflies.

"I just can't endure a woman who is bad," she said frequently—especially when there were men to listen—"even in a moving picture play. There's no reason why a girl can't stay good. No reason whatsoever."

She was fond of announcing, too, that she was good, and no man could make her any different. Yes, she knew some women traded their virtue for success, for even a chance at success. But she believed such women really had no virtue to exchange.

Madelynn was older than she looked. You might have thought her a school girl. And you knew instantly, when you saw her in the semi-private pools which dot the film colony, that this little brunette was as shapely as they make them. Slender, and yet well-rounded, with solid, cup-like breasts which added mounds of beauty and "eye-appeal" to any bathing suit in silk or wool she chose to wear. A flat stomach that went with her youth, and gracefully curved, luscious thighs.

Yet, withal, if you were even half observant, you would note her sweet devotion to her mother, and perhaps comment upon it.

"I just dread the time I will have to leave her," she would say. "Of course I will marry some time, and be a mother. I believe all women should have children—that is, of course, all married women. But he must be a real man to make me give up my career."

Sometimes she played little bits at the Silverstein studio—nice roles that were not too difficult. But mostly she was of the type known as atmosphere."

It was hard work. There were so many directors who were brusque with her; so many who looked at her "in the most evil way, mama"; so many whom she simply couldn't endure.

Some weeks she and mama lived well. Some days she was well able to spend money for a body massage by Jacques, and, though she enjoyed this physical contact with the cinema colony's chiropractor, there never was anything more to it than stripping and taking a legitimate treatment. All this cost money, but then the wasp was determined to succeed. Some weeks they could afford new clothes. Some days they knew hunger—and then the wasp would wonder how it would feel to warm herself by the flames.

But always she

"Ben," she said, "give me a thousand dollars."

hoped for the one man. He must be rich. He must be a bachelor. Divorced men often had to pay alimony. There was Thurlow Conway, for instance. Extremely fascinating. It would be a social triumph to capture him. But he divided his salary with four former wives, and his mistress, strange as it seems, was burlesque's most famous strip-tease dancer. Madelynn had never been to a burlesque show; that is, before she went to Hollywood.

Always she hoped; for she remembered mama's little saying:

"A rich husband is far better for any girl than a love-sick director; and if you give your husband a child you can do what you like."

Ben Fleet was a bachelor. He was not young, but he was rich. He was the first and the best of the moving picture bad men; the most famous of the two-gun heroes of the wide open spaces of Hollywood.

EVERYBODY knew he had made $6,000,000 for Al Wayne. Everybody knew that Silverstein paid him $5,000 a week. And everybody said it was time that Ben was marrying some nice girl.

It was easy to meet Ben. He was kind even to the extras. It was easy to talk to him—about his love for horses, his love for Indians, his days on the stage, his clever handling of guns.

And, as this story is a true one, all the facts might as well be known. It was quite easy to meet Ben's sister, Anne, with whom he resided. Madelynn was highly enthusiastic about Anne; and Anne eventually became very enthusiastic about Madelynn. She would invite her to tea; and sometimes Ben would come home early. And though he wouldn't drink tea he would be extremely gracious to Madelynn.

Sometimes he let her read his fan mail; and talked to her about some of the "regulars."

"This one," he would say, "writes me every week, telling me when to phone her. She lives in Toledo, O., has a husband and six children, and her mother. She wants to come to California.

"And this one is from an old maid school teacher in Tulsa, Okla., who always writes for money to give to charity."

Madelynn came to know them all; the nice ones, the crazy ones, the insolent ones, the adoring ones, the sarcastic and the flattering ones.

No one in Hollywood was much surprised when Ben announced his marriage to Madelynn—despite the fact that Madelynn told everybody, "it was so sudden it took my breath away."

No one was surprised to see Madelynn in furs and silks and jewels, riding in her own limousine, holding her head high when she passed old friends. No one was surprised to learn that Madelynn didn't like Ben's house, nor his furniture, nor the clothes he wore, nor even the way Anne dressed. True it was that when she did, on occasions see Anne in the nude, in the privacy of their home, she sometimes envied the sweet charm and pristine beauty of her body; but then Madelynn would take another look at herself in the tall mirror, drop off her black, lacy underthings, and realize that she wasn't at the end of the line when they handed out beauty.

Madelynn proposed to change everything to accord with their new "station in life."

No one was surprised when Ben and Madelynn separated and Madelynn let it be known that Ben was a brute and she wanted a divorce.

"She's just a gold digger," they said of her, "and Ben's woke up at last. Poor Ben!"

Yes, it was the money that separated them. It made the little wasp intoxicated. It overcame her wisdom, which was never prodigious, and inflamed her greed.

"Ben, I want a thousand dollars," she would say.

Ben would write a check.

"Ben, give me some money for mama. Poor soul, she thinks the world of you. It would be sweet of you to help her. She needs it, of course, but she'd rather cut out her tongue than say a word to you."

BEN made a trust fund whereby mama got $100 every week.

It might have gone on indefinitely, for Ben was really in love with his wife. He loved children, he loved life, and he loved Madelynn passionately—in a virile, masculine way. But the wasp made a sad mistake.

It was in the sanctity of their bedroom, two hours after dinner. Ben had taken her in his arms, on his lap, and was playing with her dark, wavy hair, and thinking that a son, or daughter, would soon be lying in the little bassinet upstairs. The perfume of her body, subtle and alluring, intoxicated him. He hugged the graceful, slender curves of her body closer; her perfectly rounded breasts, covered only by the black lace brassiere, throbbed against his vest. He had no thought in the world but love and beauty and passion.

"Ben, give me a thousand dollars," she said.

He laughed at her, gently, and twisted his finger in a curl of her raven hair.

"What do you do with all the money?" he asked.

"It's none of your business what I do with it," she cried. "Why should you ask me?" She flung herself from him. He caught her hand and held her, looking at her. He was surprised, but he made excuses. His wife's condition.

"I didn't mean to scold," he said. "But I must tell you some things so you'll understand.

"I've given you over $20,000 in a few months, besides the things I've bought for you, and they cost more than $100,000, as you know.

"I'm willing to give you all the money you need, honey, and you know it. But we can't spend so much as we have been spending; because the balance in the bank won't stand it."

"You have millions," she said, jerking her hand out of his.

"But I haven't. Everybody thinks I have, because my pictures have made so much money. I made $6,000,000 for Al Wayne, it is true. But I don't cut in on his profits; it wasn't for myself, darling. I had but $5,000 when I left him.

"Oh, honey, I'm not stingy, nor tight, nor poor. I've got enough to last you for the rest of your life—and for our baby as long as he lives. But we won't have it if it's spent at the rate of $10,000 a month. Don't you see?"

"You'll give me all the money I want," she said, "and when I want it. Or I'll tell the whole world you beat me. Why do you think I married you? For your beauty? You fool! And as for a man,—well, there

(*Concluded on page* 86)

S. O. S. Hollywood

No place is too far, no town too small —Hollywood stars must be had—at all costs!

By ROBERT DAILEY

MANNING PIERCE, a c e features man for Carmachial Pictures Ltd., sat in a small cantina in Managua, Nicaragua, and wished something would happen. It was hot and the trip on the Pan-American tri-motored plane from Hollywood had been tiring. Without enthusiasm he sipped his tepid beer and watched the crowd of native pleasure seekers. A native hostess, clad only in a width of cloth that partially covered her brown body from breasts to knees, minced up to Pierce's table and sat down beside him. He looked her over without a great deal of enthusiasm. Her skin was too dark and her teeth didn't look any too well cared for.

"You like me, no?" she queried with a provocative twist of her supine body.

"Check," grunted Pierce. "I like you no. Beat it."

The native girl seized his hand and placed it beneath her single garment on her voluptuous breast. It was warm and full and soft and the brown nipple stood out as though daring him to do his worst. The native girl was very close and he could hear her sharp breathing and feel the delectable softness of her body, but the odor of her body was there also and his passion fires refused to kindle. Abruptly he drew away from her.

"Scram," he told her shortly. "I don't like you."

The black-haired girl moved away flirting the short tail of her skirt at him disdainfully. And Pierce again resumed his contemplation of the crowded cantina. But not for long.

A lithe, evil looking fellow with a dark skin and slant eyes, whom Pierce took to be the manager, stepped upon the orchestra platform in the front of the cantina and waved for silence. Pierce sensed the wave of anticipatory joy that swept over the ordinarily unruly crowd and was sure that something unusual was about to happen.

"As I have promised you," the sour faced one began in Spanish, "you are about to see the Senorita Alverez, from Hollywood, in her famous dance, Love of the Twin Virgins."

The fellow stepped down from

trip was to visit the better cantinas of Central and South America in an effort to secure a certain type of Spanish dancer for Carmachial's new picture, *Equatorial Passions,* and he had a hunch that he might see something interesting. At least he was overlooking no bets.

the platform, there was a roar of approval and the lights went out. The stringed orchestra took up the haunting strains of a blood stirring native air and a single blue light shone in front of the cantina.

Pierce felt interested for the first time in that very dull evening. His purpose in making the long plane

SUDDENLY in front of the single light appeared a flitting, wraith-like feminine form. At first glance she appeared completely nude but he soon saw that her single garment was a swirling transparent cape. In the tempo of the rhumba she moved her sinuous body in a suggestive gesture of hesitant surrender. Her movements were now resolute, now fearful; the virgin's first affair. But as the tempo of the rhumba increased so did the fervor and confidence of the dancer. And as she moved and whirled Pierce leaned still farther forward, his pulse beating wildly and his breath coming in short gasps.

The breathtaking beauty of the girl was unbelievable. He had yet to get a better view of her features but Nature could not, he felt, be so cruel as to attach an unsightly face to such a perfect body. Beginning at her ankles he searched every inch of her body for the flaw that he hoped he wouldn't find. Trim ankles led smoothly into perfect calves that in turn flowed into symmetrically beautiful thighs. Her curving thighs and the hollows of her abdomen were unbroken by even so much as a thin scanty. Then, as his searing gaze reached the perfect twin mounds of her delectable breasts he knew that he had found the faultless female. With every movement of her mincing steps those breasts swayed and tossed, twin cone-shaped love muscles, seeming to beckon, to entreat the encroachment of a male's caress.

AND Manning Pierce, the Hollywood sophisticate, who saw girls in every state of *déshabille* every working day, was stirred almost beyond the realms of sanity.

Suddenly the lights flashed on and Pierce found that he was standing, breathing hard, gasping, holding out his arms to the bronze beauty. And just as he would have cried for surcease from the throes of passion that the delectable feminine form had awakened within him the sudden lighting of the stage all but floored him. If he had thought she was tops in feminine pulchritude in the semi-darkness, he now felt that she was unreal. Black, straight hair hung long to perfect shoulders, framing aquiline Spanish features with eyes that looked out as large pools of black onyx.

And, for the first time, Manning Pierce noted something else. The dark eyes were twin signals of distress, an S. O. S. for assistance. And Pierce saw that the black orbs were searching for something. For what? Perhaps for someone who could rescue her. From what? And instantly Pierce knew that something was wrong. Why should a girl like that be dancing in a place like this? He would, somehow, find the answer to that question.

And then, with a certainty that left him breathless, Manning Pierce knew something else. Cost what it might he must have this girl. Never would he be satisfied until he had tasted of her charm. Moving as though to applaud, he arose, catching her roving, terror-filled eyes. He saw the dark eyes rest upon him and he beckoned surreptitiously to her.

A new charm came to the set smile on her dark face as she swirled toward him, veered toward a leering villain at Pierce's right and as quickly whirled away, to approach more closely Pierce's table. Directly in front of his table she ended her Dance of the Twin Virgins, with such a passionate, pleading, caressing gesture of surrender and exotic bliss that Pierce stood and reached for her. Then she turned and bowed to the thunder of applause, escaped a brown arm that reached covetously for her bronzed body and leaned over Pierce's table.

"You were—" began Pierce, but the words stuck in his throat. The twin hemispheres of her breasts sprouted directly in front of his face, covered only by the sheer material of her cloak that was more revealing than concealing. Pierce gasped and little spots danced in front of his face.

"Senor," the throaty voice filtered through the haze. "Senor Pierce, you must help me."

She had called his name! The haze cleared miraculously and he was looking into her dark features, without recognition.

"How did you know my name?" he queried in surprise.

The dark haired dancer was gasping in sheer terror.

"It does not matter," she answered hurriedly. "It was in Hollywood. Please, you must."

"Ah, Senorita Alverez," the soft menacing voice of the manager sounded back of her, "you were deevine. And you have found a friend, no? It is well. Perhaps he is a rich Americano whom you have known. Is it not so?"

Pierce arose and was about to reply but the words were cut off by the look of sheer terror and warning in the dancer's face.

"No," she gasped quickly. "No, it is not so. I do not know heem. He has merely called me to hees table. Is it not so, Senor?" She looked appealingly at Manning Pierce.

What a come off! A moment ago the girl had called his name, had appealed for help. Now she was disclaiming knowledge of his identity. The whole affair sounded screwy to him, but he was resolved to see it through. Undoubtedly the girl was terrified and needed help. So what! Was she protecting him? If so, from what or whom?

THE manager was eyeing him speculatively, waiting for Pierce to speak.

"I am from Hollywood," began Manning Pierce, "I seek just such a dancer as Senorita Alverez. I would gladly buy her contract, *if* you have one."

There was a crafty look in the manager's slant eyes as he beamed upon the features man.

"Just so," he replied. "I am Hernandez, owner and manager of the cantina," he stuck out his hand awkwardly. "Manning Pierce," mumbled the man from Hollywood as he took the cold, fish-like hand. The manager continued, "Perhaps we might meet at my poor *hacienda* tonight, it ees not long until the closing time, then we could talk of our business. Ees eet not so?"

"No, no," the dancer's gesture was filled with despair. "I do not wish to go to Hollywood. I wish to stay here. You must not let me go." She appealed to the manager, placing one small hand upon his shoulder entreatingly.

Pierce knew it was an act for he could see the loathing in her eyes as Hernandez placed a slimy hand suggestively upon one full breast. But the glitter in the manager's eyes was replaced with a crafty light.

"There ees no h a r m," he shrugged. "We can have leetle party. Then if you decide you do not wish to go—eet ees well. So?" he nodded to Pierce.

Pierce laughed as though he were enjoying the scene but his hands ached to throttle the greasy neck of the half caste.

"It is well," he nodded. "But upon one thing I must insist. Gladly will I come to your party if I may be permitted to escort the pretty Senorita Alverez," he bowed to the frightened girl.

A new look of terror came into the girl's dark eyes and she shook her head vehemently.

"No," she cried, "it cannot be. I do not wish to go with the *Senor* Pierce. Rather would I go with you alone." She turned to Hernandez her sinuous hips swaying.

Again the covetous gleam appeared in the manager's eyes and again the crafty light replaced it. He turned to the girl with ill-concealed threat in his tone.

"Eet ees well," he said. "You shall accompany Senor Pierce to the party. Later, perhaps, we may have our own leetle party."

With a smirk he waved a careless hand to Pierce and guided the girl across the floor ahead of him. And in the dancer's eyes was such a look of terrified warning that Pierce wondered if he hadn't been a little hasty in his decision to help the girl. Some very bizarre happenings, he knew, were still wont to occur in these outlandish spots. But as he watched her swaying toward a rear door he knew that there was a double motive. Never in his eventful life had he so wished to sample feminine wares.

HERNANDEZ and the girl disappeared through the rear door and Pierce watched it covertly for the half caste's return. Minutes passed and the door did not again open. Manning Pierce began to perspire freely. What was hap-

pening? The evil visaged manager could at this very moment be attacking the girl. There was no doubt that he desired her and would attack when he felt the time was ripe.

With growing anxiety and rage taking possession of him, Manning Pierce arose to start search for Tina Alverez. But at that precise moment Hernandez stalked into the room. In sudden inspiration Pierce waved to the manager to approach. With a half sneer on his dark features Hernandez walked the intervening distance.

Pierce held a banknote of large denomination suggestively in his hand, saw the manager's greedy eyes fasten upon it.

"Perhaps it would be possible for me to go to the senorita's quarters," suggested Pierce. "We have much to talk about; the terms of contract, the casting and such."

He held out the bill and the half caste's hand closed over it like the talons of a vulture.

The manager hesitated only an instant, then:

"*Si*, I shall show you to the senorita's quarters. When I close, which will not be long, for the natives must be early at work on the banana farms, we shall talk over our own business."

As Pierce followed the man to the rear he was gloating inwardly. He was to see the beautiful dancer in her rooms. Perhaps he would even. . . . Then it suddenly occurred to him that he might be in love. Love! For Manning Pierce! That he was in danger he had no doubt, though he had not yet discovered its exact source, but the thought of the Spanish girl's charms acted as a heady wine to drive the fears of his own safety into the background. Now his only interest was to see the girl and feast his eyes upon her unbelievable beauty.

Hernandez halted before a door and rapped sharply with his knuckles.

"Who is it?" came sharply from within and Pierce could detect the note of terror in her voice.

"It is I, Manning Pierce," he hastened to say. "I come to speak with you concerning the terms of our contract."

The door opened slightly and Pierce impulsively thrust his body through the opening. He was trembling. The heavy thud of the door closing meant nothing to him, he did not realize that the door was much heavier than the thin boarding that comprised the rest of the building nor did he hear the snap of the spring lock nor the gloating laugh that issued from the lips of the half caste, Hernandez.

Once inside the room he could realize only one thing, that before him stood the most delectable bit of feminine pulchritude that it had ever been his pleasure to look upon, and Manning Pierce had been places in his time.

Over the bountious curves and hollows that comprised Tina Alverez's perfect figure she had hastily thrown a thin cape. And now the cloth gaped open so that he could see glowing halves of twin globes and glimpse the coral-tipped proturberances. There was horror in her eyes as she looked speechlessly at him, with one small hand covering her throat in a gesture of despair.

"No, no," she cried. "You must not come here. You must fly. Please go away. He will kill you. For your money he will kill you. It is all part of his game, this party business. I have come to him only today for work and now I am his prisoner, his slave. He expects me to lure rich strangers to my rooms where he will kill them for their money. For myself I do not care, but you, Manning Pierce, must go away quickly."

BUT to Manning Pierce's passion-fraught brain her pleas went unheeded. He saw only the luscious bronzed breasts and the sensuously curved body that seemed to lure him on and on. And then his arms went about her and his lips sought hers, stilling her entreaties. The lips were moist and soft and warm, soon responding to the eager plying of his tongue. Answering in kind.

Gone, for both of them, was the threat of danger. Gone was every living and every inanimate thing as they clung in delicious embrace. Her body moved closer, the soft curves folding into his hardened muscles with a caressing tenacity. His hands were under the soft cloak and, suddenly, without warning, it slipped and fell to the floor in a shimmering heap. His hands moved the length of her glorious body feeling the delectable, soft, quivering, flesh beneath. Her breath was coming in short gasps and little whimpering sound issued from her plying lips.

Tenderly, firmly she grasped his head, pulled it downward and, sensing her desires, he stooped to kiss the firm exquisite breast. Her body tautened and she swayed, rocking with delirious bliss.

Pierce caught her up in his arms knowing that he could no longer endure the rapturous joys of waiting. Blindly he stumbled with his radiant

The native girl flung herself into the room, a short dirk in her hand.

burden to a low settee that graced one side of the almost bare room. Gently he settled her and she drew him toward her. Her arms were about his neck, her lips caressing his face, her warm breath fanning the flames of passion brighter.

"Oh, Senor," she panted, "I have seen you in Hollywood, I have loved you always. There you would not notice me so I ran away. Senor...."

The last was a sigh as his hand slid down over her quivering abdomen and bosom.

"Tina, dear one," he breathed. "I'll never let you go."

"Veree pretty," a harsh voice sounded from the doorway accompanied by a sneering laugh. "Veree pretty. It ees great fun, no? And now I shall have my fun."

THERE was a scream from Tina as Manning Pierce came heavily to his feet, heavily like one who has been drugged, such havoc had passion played upon him. Quickly anger and frustrated desire replaced the lassitude of passion. He took a threatening step toward the half caste.

"What are you dong in here, in Tina's room, you dirty rat! Get the hell out of here!"

"So." Hernandez' evil lips drew back in a snarl. His right hand came up holding an automatic. "Do not approach or I shall put a bullet through your gringo heart. I shall trouble you to drop your wallet to the floor, slowly, then — we shall see." He leered evilly at Tina who was cringing upon the settee.

Manning Pierce cursed himself for not bringing a gun. He had known that danger sometimes lurked in the native cantinas. Since there was nothing better to do he reached for his inside pocket under the menacing muzzle of the half caste's automatic. There might be a chance for a break! He would play for

the shroud of unconsciousness enveloped him peacefully.

NECESSITY for action brought Pierce quickly out of his coma, only to find that his hands were tied and that he had been tossed in the corner. Through a fog of pain he looked for Tina. She was there. Upon the settee. But now her enchanting loveliness was held firmly in the grasp of the smirking half caste who seemed to be waiting for something. There was evidence of a struggle and her bronze flesh bore the marks of brutal handling.

"Ah, so you have awakened and are ready for the show," mocked Hernandez as Pierce stirred. "Later I shall slit your evil gullet and throw you in the lake; I would not care to have the comandante find blood stains here when a search is made

---

Would you like to have another red-hot, fast-moving movie action story by Robert Dailey, author of "S. O. S. Hollywood?"

---

that! Play it for all it was worth!

As the wallet dropped to the floor the manager's greedy eyes followed the course of its falling and Manning Pierce was upon him. He aimed a hurried blow at the man's face and reached for the gun arm with his other hand. The gun fired, the bullet went wild and the nimble half caste stepped quickly aside from the blow. As Pierce's body shot past off balance, Hernandez stepped back. There was a thud and a myriad of stars as the barrel of the automatic landed. A red curtain settled in front of Pierce's eyes and he knew that the floor was coming up to meet him and that he could do nothing about it. As he fell he heard a shrill scream from Tina and then

for your body. But before that we must have our little party," he guffawed loudly. "No doubt you will enjoy the leetle pastime, but not half so much as I."

Tina screamed as his talon-like hands clawed at her voluptuous breasts. Pierce raged and swore, straining at his bonds, but they held securely as the half caste threw his weight upon Tina bearing her back upon the settee. His hands played over her and when she screamed a heavy palm descended upon her mouth, bringing blood.

"You dirty scum," roared Pierce, "I'll break every bone in your body."

There was no answer from Hernandez who was bending every effort to frustrate Tina's tigerish efforts to escape. And then as his hand descended upon her cheek she fell back exhausted with pain and fatigue. A fiendish chuckle escaped the half caste as his greedy eyes feasted upon her as though stripping the bronze flesh from her body. His face was that of a vulture that picks the delectable spot before descending for the kill.

There was a sudden commotion as the door was flung open and the native girl, who had tried to entice Pierce earlier in the evening, bounded into the room. A short dirk was in her hand as she headed for Hernandez, screaming in Spanish:

"You vile son of a snake. I kill you. You shall not make her your mistress to throw me aside."

As she flung her savage body at Hernandez he twisted about catching the uplifted wrist and causing the dirk to go spinning across the room, *beneath Pierce's threshing legs.* Lifting her as he would have lifted an old shoe, the half caste threw her to the floor, gibbering and mouthing in maniacal rage. She screamed as she hit the floor and Hernandez was upon her, smashing in her face with his heavy shoe. Then with a wild laugh he turned back to Tina.

Meanwhile Pierce was working as he had never worked in his life. An inch at a time he moved the knife under his body until it was beneath his fettered hands. He had little fear of Hernandez who was fondling the nude body of Tina, but he must hurry or he would be too late.

With the knife beneath him he moved painfully back and forth, wincing with pain when its sharp blade cut into his flesh, but joying when he knew it was severing the strands of the rope. At last one hand came loose and he could hardly

restrain the triumphant yell that welled in his throat. But not until he had carefully cut away the fetters from the other hand and had flexed his muscles did he move. He had already tried the strength and agility of the half caste.

Like a tornado gone animate, Manning Pierce hurled his big body across the room to fall upon the half caste. The desire to kill, to rend bone and muscle with the strength of his own hands was strong upon him and he cast the dirk away. Catching the man around the neck he shook him until his teeth rattled and his swarthy features mottled purple then, still holding him with his left, he drew back his right and let fly again and again, joying in the crunch of bone as his fist landed in the man's evil face.

WHEN Hernandez was a limp rag he threw him to one side, terrible, animal-like joy surging within him as he heard the crunch of bone when the greasy head hit the wall.

Then he turned to Tina, lifting her, covering her face with kisses. A sob left him as her eyelids fluttered, opened.

"Tina, my darling," he cried. "It is I. Everything's all right. I'm taking you away from this hell hole."

"Gracious Dios," she whispered as she replied to his warm kisses.

His berth in the tri-motored plane was ready for them when they arrived at the airport, and all the joys of a good, wide world awaited them in the future.

The Spanish dancer for Carmachial Pictures, Ltd.? Well, he might let them have her for one picture, but no more. By the oldest law of mankind she was his own. Finders keepers.

It Happened in

Loyalty to her film company came first—after her husband. A clever story with a surprise ending

By LARS ANDERSON

VITAMOUNT Pictures' big lot was curiously silent and deserted that morning. The few persons to be seen were hurrying through their tasks with a set purpose in mind. For at ten o'clock, on sound stage twenty-eight, Director Lew Fitzwaters was to shoot the bath-tub sequences required for the much heralded extravaganza for private showing. *Hot Society*, starring Maureen Russell.

Of course, it was a well-known fact about the studio that the haughty La Russell was not to actually appear in the *risque* scenes. To intimates, the actress confided that she wouldn't consider such de-

HOLLYWOOD

grading exposure of her charms for the amusement of the moronic *hoi polloi*. However, the truth of the matter was that her somewhat shop-worn charms would not fit in well, in the altogether, in view of the glamorous role she was portraying in the society opus!

So the studio forces, to a man, knew that Dawn O'Shea, young and shapely "stand-in" for Maureen, was to disrobe for the desired "shots." Thus, the intense excitement. For the lovely Dawn was considerable female in any man's picture, or out of it, for that matter.

Promptly at ten, absolute silence reigned over the huge sound stage designated as No. 28, as a brilliant battery of kleigs were snapped into blazing life. The set was arranged to resemble a sumptuous bath, in modernistic black and silver. Three

A brassiere covered her firm breasts.

big, square-eyed cameras were tilted at intriguing angles toward a luxurious sunken tub on one side of the room, and a cameraman manned each of them. Alf Welbon, chief cameraman, conversed in low tones with the director, nearby.

THE eager crowd numbered fully a hundred. Among them were actors, make-up artists, hoofers, scenarists, stenographers, electricians, prop men, and— But why go on? Vitamount's entire staff was out in full force to witness the climax of the extravaganza which had been planned for months, and to see the unveiling of the beautiful "bit" girl whose loveliness topped that of the glamorous La Russell!

As the lights clicked on, Fitzwaters advanced to meet Dawn O'Shea who had stepped from the wings, her luscious figure swathed in a terry-cloth robe of snowy white. Her hard, conical breasts, like toothsome pears with bulbous tips, pushed the upper part of the robe out into twin tents of delight. Soft, butterhued hair streamed about her shoulders in a perfect blend with the blue of her great eyes. Blue Empire slippers completed her ensemble.

"You're not nervous?"

Dawn smiled at the director's question. Two seasons with the Nudities had cured her of any nervous qualms as far as the revealment of her lovely body for amusement purposes was concerned.

"I'm ready," she answered simply.

"Atta girlie!" grinned Fitzwaters. "Now, you enter from the end door, saunter slowly forward, disrobe and enter the tub. Hum, sing, do anything, as long as you appear natural and nonchalant. Clear?"

She nodded, turned and walked through the open door at the far end of the bathroom.

"Camera! This is the take, Alf."

The sound mechanism was then switched on and camera flywheels spun industriously as the director sank into a chair alongside Welbon's camera. As though in the privacy of her own bath, Dawn stepped out almost in full view of the expectant audience. Her lithe grace was the personification of nonchalance as she prepared to doff the concealing robe. She softly hummed a bar from the *Kishmiri Song*. With her make-up skillfully applied, she was truly a remarkable double for the missing star, although her loveliness of figure distinctly shaded that of the older woman.

Stripping the robe from about her slender body, and stepping from the slippers, Dawn stood forth in tempting and lovely view. From the top of her gleaming head to the tips of her tiny, tinted toes, she was the acme of alluring femininity. Dimpled curves and sweeping lines predominated with twin breasts standing forth from her soft chest with such amazing rigidity as to cause the spectators to wonder if they had not been placed upon her as an afterthought! As the coolish air of the set touched their tight-skinned contours, the salmon-tinted nipples hardened and stood forth, temptingly.

Between those twin charms, a flat youthful torso swept downward into a v-shaped valley of compelling allure. Generous hips, full, firm-fleshed thighs melted into dimpled knees and slender calves in a perfect symphony of graceful rhythm. As she tossed her head, the sheen of her golden hair scintillated with a million rays as the brilliant incandescents high-dived into its soft tousled tresses. A transparent brassiere covered her firm breasts.

Dawn hesitated a moment for effect. Then, with infinite grace, she entered the sunken tub. As Fitzwaters had coached her, she arranged her gorgeous body in such a way as to afford the necessary concealment from the grinding cameras.

For long moments, she lazed in the warm, scented comfort of the bath. Stretching at full length, she agitated the water at her sides, watched the tiny waves slide over the salmon crests of her upright breasts, roll down her soft, flat stomach and rejoin the water at her hips. Gently she rubbed a huge bar of soap between her palms and spread the thick white lather over her body, massaging the creamy crystals into the solid swell of the wondrous, tight-skinned treasures that adorned her milky-white chest.

At a silent signal from Fitzwaters Dawn emerged from the bath, posed nonchalantly behind a transparent screen in shadowy and lovely nakedness. Her perfect figure gleamed rosily in the glow of the lights as she wielded a heavy towel, the toothsome nipples of her snowy breasts again rising into tempting prominence as the coarse fabric touched them. Then her dainty feet were again encased in the slippers, the robe concealed her magnificent body, and she had disappeared from view. A mighty burst of applause went up in her wake as the sound mechanism was switched off, but she did not reappear in answer to it.

SAM WERMUTH, production chief, looked very dignified sitting behind an orderly mahogany desk. He leaned back in his swivel chair, folded pudgy hands over a hefty paunch, nodded Dawn O'Shea to a heavily unholstered chair beside him.

"So," he grunted, "you're Dawn O'Shea?"

Dawn studied him without appearing to do so. He was short and fat, and, she guessed, about fifty. His blunt-fingered hands beat an incessant tattoo upon the desk as he leaned toward her, his small eyes playing over her figure, appraisingly. His eyes made her feet momentarily unclothed. She dropped her glance, looking up only when he addressed her again.

"So you think you can act?" he demanded harshly.

Dawn colored slightly. "Haven't I proven it, Mr. Wermuth?" she questioned, softly.

The production man smiled. "Proven it? How? Surely, you do not consider the bathing sequences as dramatic triumph? Any shapely girl might have carried that off successfully, given the same coaching that you received. You were chosen because of a peculiar resemblance to Miss Russell, and you followed instructions well. Other than that, you've proven nothing, Miss O'Shea."

"That—why—that is not wholly true, Mr. Wermuth," she bravely managed. "And I could prove my ability to you if I were given the chance—" She broke off, half-rose as though to leave, but he waved her to her seat again.

"I like your spirit," he confessed, half-grudgingly. "And I feel inclined to give you the chance you desire. Wait!" he continued, quickly, as Dawn's piquant face brightened, perceptibly. "Don't expect a break before the camera until you have proven yourself."

Dawn felt a deep scarlet color surging into her smooth cheeks.

"Just what do you mean?" she asked, instantly suspicious.

"Not what you evidently think, my dear," grinned Wermuth, easily. "It is merely that I want you to try something our entire staff of agents have failed in accomplishing. It's the signing of Lyle d'Estrel, the French dramatic star, to a Vitamount contract—"

"But—that is—I don't see—" began Dawn, but he broke in.

"Cinema, Incorporated, just about has the Frenchman cinched," he said enviously. "But we'll go to any lengths to sign him, long term. All the he-men have failed us; perhaps a good-looking girl like yourself can swing it." He looked at her expectantly.

"But—how—" she stammered, momentarily nonplussed.

Wermuth frowned. "Women are supposedly ingenious; actresses are supposed to be able to act convincingly. Well, you're undeniably a most charming woman, and you claim you can act. Do I make myself clear?"

Dawn considered a moment.

"And if I succeed, Mr. Wermuth?" she ventured softly.

"You'll be given a leading role in _Broadway Cocktail_," he rejoined. "And a nice bonus besides. Fair enough?"

She laughed devilishly. "He's as good as hooked right now," she boasted. "So make out the contract, and get your checkbook ready. Little Dawn is one girl who always gets her ham."

Before Dawn O'Shea had landed with the Nudities, she had led a life of comparative ease and luxury. Three years at one of the best East-ern finishing schools, a blissful year abroad and then—bang!—the O'Shea fortune was shattered into a million pieces, each too small and scattered to bother collecting. For the first time in her life, Dawn was forced to provide for herself.

She had been motherless from infancy, and the shock of losing his fortune had proven too much for her elderly father. He had died a few weeks after the disastrous October of '29, leaving her utterly alone. But the shapely Dawn had faced the situation with dauntless courage. Cars, clothing, and jewels had gone to satisfy unpaid creditors. An old friend of the family had secured her a first engagement in the chorus. She fell right into the swing of the work. Possessed of something unusual in the way of loveliness of face and figure, it was not long until she was doing a specialty with the celebrated Nudities.

All that was behind her now. When she had left the stage and journeyed westward to Hollywood, she felt as though, once and for all, she was done with showing her undraped body for amusement purposes. She dreamed of gradually gaining recognition in pictures, earning herself a worthy spot among the actresses of filmdom.

However, she had been doomed to disappointment. Hollywood wanted her for her body, and paid her well for exposing it to the cameras, but never a chance was offered whereby she might triumph as an actress alone.

THE next three days were busy ones for the little "bit" girl. She leased a costly apartment near that of Lyle d'Estrel's, moved into it, and purchased enough extravagant raiment at Billock's Wiltshire to suitably gown the queen of a realm—undies, frothy with lace—negligees, soft and satiny — hose, cobwebby and sheer—glittery jewelery — exotic perfumes — luxurious furs—expensive gowns that reflected all the elegance and glamor that is high fashion. As yet she had formulated no definite plan of campaign for ensnaring the French actor, but she did not believe in penny-pinching or halfway measures. Dawn felt that her chance would inevitably come and, when it did, she did not intend to fail through any fault of her own.

On the third day after Sam Wermuth's proposition, Dawn entered her apartment in mid-afternoon, after spending several wearying hours at the studio while Alf Welbon shot countless "stills" for the publicity department. Tossing her tiny chapeau to the bed in her boudoir, she crossed the deep-piled *Roneau* and looked across the court. And instantly, she snapped to attention.

In the opposite wing of the building, thirty feet away, Opportunity was beckoning. Her blue eyes widened as inspiration swept over her. *Her Golden Opportunity!*

A man was sunning himself on the tiny porch there, sprawled in an easy chair. He was rather tall, with broad shoulders and wavy black hair. His eyes were shaded by dark glasses.

Lyle d'Estrel! Dawn was sure she recognized him from the many pictures she had seen in the newspapers at the time of his arrival in Hollywood. Yet in person he seemed twice as handsome as he had in the photographs! It would be far from distasteful to fence with this handsome foreigner, try to win him over

to Vitamount Pictures, and, at the same time, earn herself a contract and the princely bonus.

Dawn hesitated but a moment. Then, with slender fingers that trembled, she undressed, doing so blushingly inasmuch as the act was accomplished within full view of the watching man. Of course, she had exposed her charms from the stage, and before the cameras many times, but somehow this was entirely different.

STANDING teasingly close to the window, she grasped her backless crepe frock, pulled it slowly upward, disclosing her beautiful legs and dimpled knees, gleaming in sheer, cobwebby silk. The dress continued slowly upward under the pull of her fingers to where silk ended and creamy flesh began.

Bare thighs gleamed not unlike polished ivory in the reflected sunlight from the big window. They were perfect models of tapered beauty. Her hips were lusciously full as they slid tantalizingly into view, yet delicately rounded and curved. Up—up—up passed the frock over a flat youthful torso, the lines gracefully swelling into breasts that were snowy mounds of glorious beauty.

Then it came off over her shining head and Dawn stood disclosed, a figure of sheer loveliness, clad in nothing more serviceable than gossamer hose, and the most abbreviated of lacy briefs.

Slyly, she glanced at her prospective audience of one in the tall pier glass. He had discarded the dark glasses and was leaning forward in the chair with hypnotic rigidity. Smiling saucily to herself, Dawn bent down and peeled the wispy

Dawn wasn't sure whether the man across the court had seen her or not. She hoped he hadn't.

stockings from her shapely legs. Straightening, she slid her slim fingers beneath the elastic waistband of the tiny briefs, pushed them downward over satin thighs to her knees. An abrupt little movement with her feet, and Dawn stood lusciously, temptingly naked before the window.

For several delightful moments she moved about before the mirror. She pirouetted coquettishly, holding her slender hands beneath her swelling breasts, raising them even higher than their natural formation readily permitted. Then she released them and studied them in the glass, and there was not even a hint of a droop marring their rotund magnificence. Salmon crested and pert, they stood straight out from her chest in proud, glorious beauty.

A PROVOCATIVE smile curved Dawn's bee-stung lips as she envisaged the almost certain effect this daring display must be having on her neighbor. She poised herself and began dabbing at her five feet, four, of delicious nudity with a large pink puff. With teasing slowness, she moved this way and that, and assumed many different postures while powdering her sleek, satiny loveliness.

A born actress, she carried the entire performances off with an air of unselfconsciousness that would have done full justice to the famous Maureen Russell herself. Presently she covered her more tempting charms with sheer, silken step-ins, slipped her tiny pink-toed feet into blue suede slippers and drew on a silken kimona of blue. Then, she left the window.

Dawn had just reclined on the divan with a cigarette when the doorbell jangled, insistently. She smiled impishly as she crushed the cigarette in a convenient tray and went to answer the summons. She felt sure that it would be her good-looking neighbor calling.

She opened the door a crack, peeped out. A tall, handsome stranger, dark and wide-shouldered, stood there smiling, hat in hand. *Lyle d'Estrel!*

"Good evening, *Mam'selle* Des Bordes?" he questioned, softly.

"No," Dawn hugged the kimona closely about her bare body. "There is no one here by that name."

She acted as though she were going to close the door, but the man moved closer, his captivating eyes flitting over her in frank admiration that Dawn found rather disconcerting, although not unpleasant. He was, she quickly decided, a most fascinating person, and well worth cultivating had there been no ulterior motives in her mind.

"*Mais,* I thought I might find *Mam'selle* Des Bordes," he smiled, flashing his white teeth. "And I thought to continue an old acquaintance begun in Paris long ago. However, if you will not mind, I would like to talk with you who are so charming. Being a stranger in a strange land is not what it might be, I can assure you! My name is d'Estrel . . . Lyle d'Estrel of Paris, France. . . ."

DAWN'S appraising eyes missed no detail of his clean-cut profile, his tall, broad-shouldered handsomeness of figure and the manner that fairly radiated tremendous power.

A moment later the foreigner was in her living room. After learning her name, he kept up a continual flow of sophisticated talk which left Dawn at ease to study him closely. A firm chin, well-shaped lips and frank grey eyes were attractive features of his healthy, tanned face. She judged him to be about thirty-five, rather younger than she had thought he would be, but even more compelling in a suave, masculine way.

Knowingly, she focused the entire power of her dynamic eyes on him, permitting them to smile engagingly and narrow languorously

at will. She sensed his own vision centered on her pouting breasts, traveling by slow degrees down her quivering body in a frank caress. She finally spoke:

"Might I offer you a drink, Mr. d'Estrel?" she asked, temptingly.

He accepted, momentarily lifting his eyes from the deep, velvety valley between her lovely breasts that s h o w e d quite plainly where the silken kimono s t o o d revealingly open. His eyes were frank with visual compliment.

"*Oui, merci, Mam'selle,*" he smiled enthusiastically.

Dawn moved to get a bottle and glasses, undulating her gorgeous hips voluptuously as she walked. His eyes assured her of complete victory as she returned to his side. She poured him a man's-sized drink which he downed appreciatively after a test sip.

"What a lovely apartment you have," he remarked, though his dark eyes were only for her.

"Why, yes, lovely, isn't it?" returned Dawn as she sipped at a tall glass.

"It is not nearly so lovely as it's tenant!" he ventured, boldly, his eyes boring into her flushing face.

"Are you quite sure?" teased Dawn. "Or are you merely being nice?"

"It sounds like flattery, I will admit," he smiled, "but flattery would be quite impossible without you as it's inspiration, *Mam'selle!*"

"I'll need a smoke after that one," she laughed, her white teeth flashing and eyes narrowing languorously. He echoed her laugh, produced cigarettes, and they both bent to the flame of his lighter.

"I am new here myself," he told her; then, "And I like my suite very much. Especially the view from my windows! I find that truly inspirational!"

DAWN flushed, guiltily. Things were moving a bit faster than she had anticipated! "That's—that's nice—" she stammered. She rose from the divan, poured him another drink.

As he accepted the second glass, frank admiration shone from his dark eyes as they swept over Dawn's scantily-clad figure. Truly, there was much to admire, for her exotic form was set off by the kimono with breath-taking exactness. It clung tenaciously to each gorgeous undulation of her glorious figure. When she moved the shimmering silk seemed to mold against her thighs, outlining them in detail. But what was most startling was the manner in which her perfect breasts pushed out the upper part of the clinging garment. Each movement brought a delicious little jiggle to their amazing rigidity, and caused the French-

man to wet his lips, nervously! The smooth valley between the twin charms, tender and downy, seemed to beg for the loyalty of kisses!

Abruptly, d'Estrel rose, moved close to her.

"You are adorable!" he breathed, and held out his long arms to her. Dawn melted into them, her head thrown back, her eyes half closed. Murmuring endearments, he kissed her, tenderly at first, then more fiercely as a rising tide of emotion swept him. Nor could Dawn remain passive for long. She returned his ardent embraces, met his eager caresses with a savage intensity of her own. Almost beside himself with desire, the Frenchman lifted her in his arms.

"Wait, Lyle! Stop!" She pushed against his steel-muscled chest with tiny, flower-like hands.

He hesitated, p l a i n l y puzzled. "Dawn, my sweet, I love you!" His tone bespoke his eager desire.

"Please, Lyle, let me down," she pleaded.

He released her, drew a deep breath of baffled desire. She turned, glided toward the bedroom. At the door, she paused, smiled at him, her own desire heavy in her breast.

"I must get into something else," she cooed, "and then I'll be back."

Lyle d'Estrel paced restlessly up and down the room. His blood was a river of fire in his veins; it was impossible for him to keep still.

After a time, he lifted his head and listened. He could hear Dawn as she moved about in the bedroom. He hesitated for a moment, then turned and strode in the direction of the sounds!

Dawn let out an alarmed feminine squeal as he turned the knob and peeped in. For a moment he stood motionless in the doorway; then he stepped inside, closing the door behind him!

She was in the very act of stepping into a pair of lacy panties! Her delectable, creamy body, entirely innocent of covering, was a truly gorgeous sight! Lyle d'Estrel fairly gasped at the thrilling revelation of her exposed charms.

"You are unbelievably lovely, my darling!" One uncontrollable lunge forward, and he was beside her, crushing his hot lips to her moist mouth, feeling her perfect, throbbing breasts flatten against the hardness of his chest. The panties dropped softly to the floor as Dawn let her rounded arms coil up about his neck in delightful invitation. Quickly, he stooped and raised her glowing body in his masterful arms!

Dawn yielded herself to him, but with a quaking heart. Primarily, her only object had been to trap this man into signing a Vitamount contract, but now . . . now, something that should have been secondary was taking the place of the original plan in her heart! But, somehow, she didn't care! As in a dream, she realized that she had never experienced the emotion that now claimed her as she lay in the Frenchman's steely arms!

The latter toyed with her emotions. He would begin kissing her with little teasing kisses that did not satisfy until her arms would clasp about him in such a way as to make release impossible until she had slaked her thirst at the fount of his lips.

HOURS later, Dawn walked softly across the deep-piled rug of the living room, and switched on a tiny table lamp. Its rays gleamed rosily on her perfect shoulders. Her shimmering hair was tumbled in wild disarray, her passion-swollen lips were widely parted. As she lifted the telephone from its cradle, her blue eyes twinkled devilishly, her white teeth glistening in a smile of triumph. She spoke softly:

"Mr. Wermuth?"

"Yes," came the answer through t h e crackling diaphram of the phone. "T h i s is Mr. Wermuth speaking."

"This is D a w n O'Shea," she breathed, "and I wanted you to know that you have an engagement for three tomorrow afternoon to arrange contract details with Lyle d'Estrel. . . ."

"What?"

"Yes, it is all arranged for him to sign with Vitamount, Mr. Wermuth," she said, softly.

"Well, that's just fine," boomed the production chief, "And you can come in for your contract and bonus tomorrow afternoon, too, Miss O'Shea. Is that okay?"

Dawn laughed softly and glanced apprehensively in the direction of the sleeping chamber.

"I'm afraid that will be impossible," s h e whispered excitedly. "You see, Lyle wants me to give up pictures. We're being married in the morning, and he insists that his w i f e be non-professional. Good night, and my thanks to you, Mr. Wermuth, for bringing me this great happiness. I wanted to tell you how much I appreciated all you have done for me, and to tell you you'll never know what you've *really* done for me. Understand? . . ."

She cradled the phone on the gasping production man with a smile, and doing so, turned toward the other room.

HOLLYWOOD LOVE SHIFT

Tim Boardman falls for an attractive blonde and incidentally assists in apprehending a criminal

By FRANK KENNETH YOUNG

TIM BOARDMAN looked up from his work in the Hollywood Garage, and stared into the blue eyes of a Jean Harlowesque blonde creature with skin as soft and white as the petals of a gardenia.

"I'm in trouble!" she confided, dimpling.

Tim continued to stare, until a heavy wrench slipped from his hand and fell with a "clank" upon the cement floor. Then he awoke abruptly.

"Not surprising!" he stammered. "Did somebody try to eat you? You look tempting enough!"

"Don't be silly!" she reproved. "It's car trouble!"

"Oh!"

Tim came to life and stepped forward, his gaze held the provoking "jiggling" of jutting breasts, so apparent through the thin silk fabric that molded the youthful mounds.

"I was on my way here, this evening," the lady explained, "when I ran out of gas. Will you help me?"

Tim beamed. "I know of no better way of spending an evening," he said facetiously.

His gaze followed hers about the work room, and he saw that her arrival had played havoc among the crew. Three men had quit their tasks and started forward, all eager to wait on her! Tim yelled to Jimmy, the pump boy, to bring some gas.

The woman chuckled faintly as a staring, goggle-eyed mechanic dropped a heavy jack on his toe. She gurgled appreciatively as another let a gas tank overflow, bathing his feet and making a puddle on the floor. Then she turned toward Tim, who had opened the door of a car and was waiting for her to enter.

As she climbed over the running board, he reveled in the flash of trim, silk-dressed legs, and the bouncing of her girlish breasts as she settled back against the cushions of the front seat.

"Okay, Miss—Miss—?"

"Gordon!" she supplied. "But just call me Tana, please! . . . My car, a new sports roadster, is stalled just two blocks South." She glanced curiously at Tim. . . . "New man here?" She sensed that his eyes were trying to penetrate the silkiness of her bodice.

"Yeah—just took charge of the night shift; been on the day shift

Tim looked up into the blue eyes of a gorgeous platinum blonde

for three weeks; until tonight. . . . "

Arrived at the parked roadster, Tana hopped out without giving Tim a chance to assist her. He wondered what he could do to prolong this delightful adventure! Filling an empty gas tank offered little opportunity. Done in a jiffy and then, blooey!—a bit of heaven vanished from his life, and chances were he'd never see her again!

The job completed, he helped her into her car, and caught a ravishing glimpse of a cream-white thigh, and slender, yet beautifully curved legs. An elusive and feminingly lovely perfume reached his nostrils. His head swam. As she leaned forward to switch on lights and ignition, the low decolletage of her gown fell loosely away from her bosom, revealing a pair of satin-skinned, pink-crested hillocks—and instantly, Tim's mind was made up!

"Mind letting me ride back to the garage with you?" he asked, sliding into the seat beside her, without waiting for her reply. "I'll send a man down for my bus. I want to see how this car runs."

"We'd b e t t e r hurry," she remarked, watching him from under silky lashes. "Dave's blood pressure won't stand for much delay."

Tim's strongly chiseled face set in cold, hard lines. Just as he had feared! No danger of such a glorious creature being footloose and fancy free! There'd be nothing he'd like better than to "go to town" with her.

"Dave who?" he jerked out.

"Werner—your boss, of course!"

Tim was silent, his gaze fastened on the curve of her thigh which was moving tantalizingly in her tight dress, as she pressed and released the gas, changed a dainty foot to the brake pedal and back again.

Tana looked at him questioningly. "You don't seem pleased," she remarked. "Don't you consider me lucky? Many a girl would give her right eye to be in my place!"

"Some have even g i v e n their lives," he replied gravely. "The way of Dave Werner with a woman is common gossip in Hollywood!"

"Oh, I've heard some of the talk going around," she answered. "But —it's hard to believe. He seems so good-hearted—always jolly!"

"Yes, but a hyena too, grins while stalking its prey!"

Did she merely shrug her young, shapely shoulders; was the movement a shudder? Tim wondered.

"He's your boss," she reminded curtly.

"Your safety is worth more than my job! I'd warn any woman— especially one like you! . . . Been in Hollywood long?"

"About a month."

"Screen test?"

"Yes—a private one."

Tim's face darkened. "Thought so!" he muttered. "Undress, in Werner's sumptuous Beverly Hills home with that florid-faced, bull-necked so-and-so as the sole tester, eh?"

Tana stiffened. "R e a l l y, Mr. Garageman! I'm free, white and twenty-one—and you're not only a total stranger, but also a most disloyal employee!"

Tim leaned impulsively toward her. His hands itched to caress her heaving breasts. More lovely in her anger. Then spoke:

"Listen, Tana," he said. "I happen to know that not one of your pretty predecessors h a s survived long after submitting to a screen test! One disappeared entirely. Another died in a closed garage while trying drunkenly to drive her car out. Still another plunged to her death over a precipice! Now, will you listen?"

"No!" she retorted. "But I shall report you to Dave!"

The roadster s t o p p e d at the garage. Tim glared as he left the car, cursing himself for a jealous fool, even though all he had said was true!

BUT Tana, evidently, didn't tell Werner, for Tim remained on at the garage; and his heart did gymnastics every time Tana entered on Werner's arm. She merely flashed a meaningful smile, and turned her head away.

Three nights after the first meeting, Tim answered an insistent buzzing of the telephone.

"Hello!" cooed a low, seductive voice.

Tim's lean, young face flushed as he recognized the tones.

"Would you mind bringing Mr. Werner's car up to my apartment?" Tana asked sweetly. "He's leaving town, and it's almost traintime. Hurry!"

Tim left Jimmy in charge of the floor and raced to the "man-lift," too jittery to wait for a mechanic to bring the car down.

The "man-lift"—a carrier belt to which was attached hand bars and steps—moved up one side of the building and down the other, and was of great convenience to one in a hurry. Now, it suddenly came to an abrupt stop, and Tim jerked startled eyes upward, to find the ceiling but a few inches from his head!

"Holy Mackerel!" he exclaimed. "That was a close call! I'd better pay attention to this thing, or it'll be over the top for me!" He jumped off, bowed mockingly to the safety device, and thanked Lady Luck that it had worked!

Only two days before, one of the boys, going up in this same lift, had spied the glorious blonde on her way from her car to the passenger elevator, and had been entranced by her beauty. The sun had been at her back, revealing her lovely and shapely legs in silhouette through her thin silk dress. The result: dazed boy—near tragedy! One of the men had stopped the mechanism of the "lift" just in time!

Werner's garage manager had ruled that, henceforth, Tana would be attended only by the foreman in charge. Ben Turner, gruff, surly tireman, had offered to remain on the night shift indefinitely, and when refused the privilege, his displeasure had been most evident. . . .

Finally, arrived at the seventh floor, Tim climbed into the "old man's" shiny, sleek sedan, and swished down the ramp, faster, ever faster. The flashing posts warned him to apply brakes not only to the car but to his emotions as well! Tana certainly had him going in circles!

It was obvious that she liked him. And now that her portly lover was going on a journey, who could tell what might happen? Perhaps he might even persuade her to "ditch"

Werner for him!—if he wasn't already too late. His heart sank at the thought. He didn't want Werner's leavings! But, no; T a n a couldn't be that sort. There must be another reason for her loyalty to Werner.

TIM sped up the boulevard, barging through a red light and narrowly missing another v e h i c l e. "Damn!" he swore. "I wouldn't have dreamed that a woman could do this to me!" Guiltily, he tightened his grip on the wheel and held his gaze to the road.

"What k e p t you?" demanded Werner, when Tim arrived somewhat breathless.

"Sorry; I came as fast as I could."

"Now don't fuss!" Tana scolded, looking dangerously beautiful in a white crepe frock—and very little else. "You'll make your train in good time, darling!"

"Darling!" Tim snorted under his breath. Then she really was— oh, hell, why did he have to be such a blithering idiot about this tantalizing bundle of blonde beauty? Yet the sly smile she gave him sent his pulses galloping!

He had no idea how they reached the depot. The late evening traffic seemed hardly to exist as he guided the s o f t l y purring car skillfully through the maze. He was angry enough with the world to have driven through Hades without a burn!

He dared not treat himself to even one glance at Tana through the rear view mirror. But as she chatted gaily, he could not help thrilling to the sound of her voice, though he gritted his teeth in the effort.

Her deep-voiced companion seemed

in happy mood, and his rumbling remarks, from time to time, chilled Tim's heart. . . .

"Well, here we are!"

Tim purposely and a bit spitefully brought the car up with a bump against the curb at the railway station, and was surprised when his portly employer appeared only pleased.

"Umph!" Werner grunted. "That's the sort of driving I like to see! You made good time, my boy!" His round face fairly beamed as he descended from the car.

"Thank you. Anything else, sir?"

"No, Boardman. Here comes a man after my bags."

Werner and Tana made their way into the crowd, leaving Tim to wait for Tana's return.

After a few minutes, Tana tripped daintily back, getting in the way of two burly "flat foots" who were hurrying forward. She accepted their clumsy apologies with a smile, and hurried on to the waiting car. Her face was flushed with excitement, as she flung her little white hat into the rear seat.

"Oh, say!" she gasped, attracted by an object on the floor. "Dave forgot the most important part of his baggage—his brief case! Oh, Tim, will you see if you can overtake him? And be sure to hand it to HIM, personally?"

WERNER had boarded the train, and Tim was obliged to battle his way through the crowd. A thin man heavily bundled and oddly familiar, cursed hoarsely as Tim brushed past him. But there was no time for formalities. Tim burst unceremoniously into Werner's private compartment.

"Here's your—" he began, then stopped. "Oh-oh!" he gasped at glimpse of the scene before him.

A mixture of feminine legs, lacy lingerie and masculine hands seemed all entangled with soul kisses and the promise of warmer weather ahead!

Tim mopped his forehead and blinked. "I beg your pardon," he said. "I thought I was on a train, not in a— Well, anyway, here's your brief case, Mr. Werner!"

The partially disrobed and decidedly voluptuous brunette slipped abruptly from the lap of the swel-

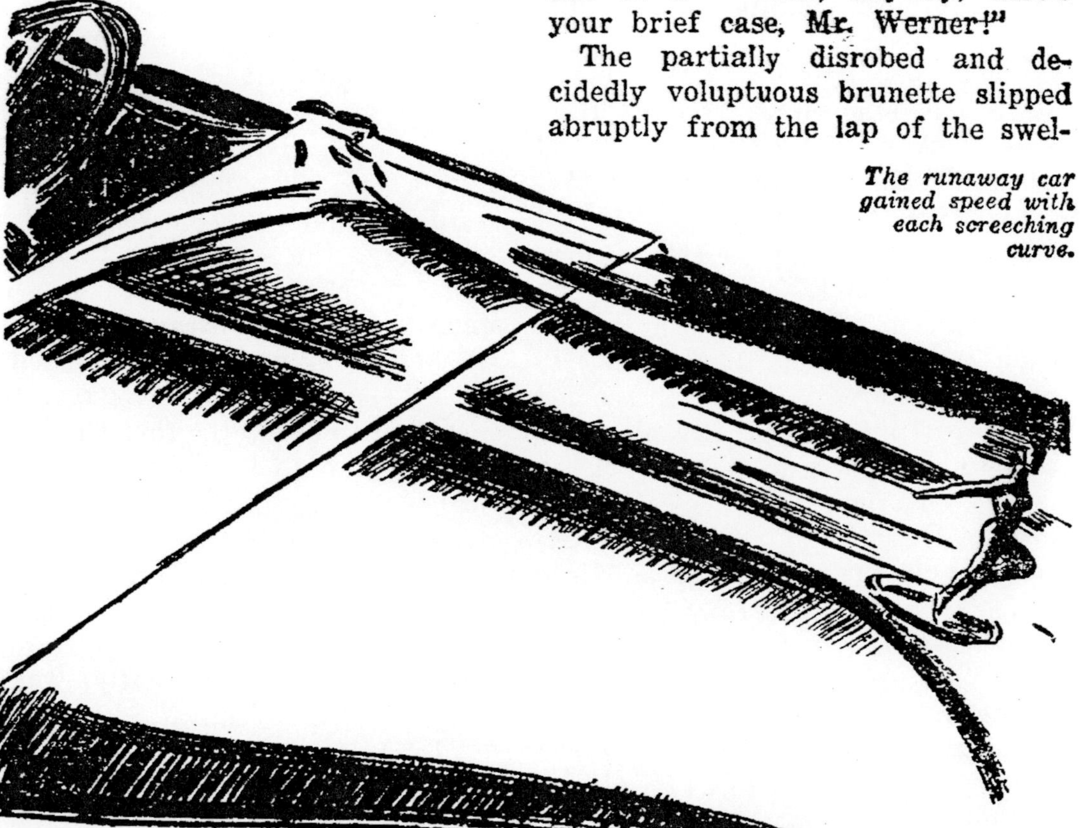

The runaway car gained speed with each screeching curve.

tering Werner, and the fat man rumbled a curse as he leaped to his feet. His flabby face changed expression quickly as his beady eyes fell upon the leather case in Tim's hand.

"Oh—ah, yes, the brief case!" He coughed to conceal his embarrassment. "Thank you! Er—thank you very much, Boardman! Here is something for your trouble!"

Tim's lips curled as he accepted the five-spot and glanced from the pleading eyes of the older man to the "torrid tootsie" somewhat arrogantly arranging her attire.

"Thank *you*, Mr. Werner!" Tim backed out, closing the door with exaggerated politeness and discretion.

The train had already begun to move. Tim leaped from the steps just as one of the burly men whom ~~he had seen~~ bump into Tana, climbed aboard.

A S HE reached the sedan, Tana flashed a dazzling smile and asked: "Well, did you catch him?"

"And how!" Tim snarled. "I wish you had been along to get an eyeful for yourself!"

He slid in behind the wheel, and Tana settled herself comfortably in the front seat with him. He seemed to be getting the breaks all of a sudden, for she leaned a bit closer as he snapped on the ignition switch. He pressed the starter button, and as the shift lever slid into low, his hand accidentally contacted a warm firm, rounded thigh.

She wriggled still closer while tuning in the radio. The soft, resilient mound of one breast pressed lightly against his arm. Tim almost lost control of himself and the car, too! He barely managed to negoti-

ate the curve ahead and turn into the seashore road with its fifty-foot precipice dropping down sheer on one side.

Tana Gordon laughed deliciously, smoothing her hair back from her white brow. "What makes you so nervous?" she asked teasingly.

His dark, glowing eyes swerved swiftly. "I wonder," he said meaningly.

"Would you rather I moved into the rear seat?"

"What do you think?"

"I think you'd feel better if you knew what I know!" she said mysteriously.

"And that goes double!"

"Meaning?"

"You should have delivered that brief case, and seen what your boy friend was doing!"

"He's not my boy friend," was the surprising retort. "Whatever he's up to wouldn't astonish me, and whatever it is, it can't last long!"

"Oh, no?" Tim was feeling reckless.

She turned squarely toward him.

"What's the use of our talking at cross purposes?" she asked. "I'm almost bursting with good news! So, here's the story! I've wanted to tell you ever since the night I first met you, but until the time was right, I had to hold my tongue!"

"I don't get it," he said bewilderedly. "What's the idea?"

"Do I look like a G-man?"

Tim laughed at the unexpected question. Then he became serious, seeing that she, apparently, was in earnest. "Not really?"

"Temporarily."

"Werner?"

"Right; caught my man, too! Did you see those dicks I bumped into at the station? . . . That was our signal. If I collided with them, it meant Werner was on the train and everything was ready for them to act. If I passed by them haughtily, they were to lie low awhile longer."

"They boarded the train as I was getting off!"

"Certainly! There was another one inside, on guard."

"Oh, the thin man! I thought I recognized him. Now I know. He was around making inquiries after one of Werner's flames died! . . . Let me see, what was her name? . . . Mary . . . Marilyn. . . ."

"Marjorie—Marjorie Gordon!" Tana supplied in bitter tones.

"Gordon? . . . Why, not—"

"Yes; my sister! It was to avenge her death that I pretended friendship for Werner. As you said, everybody knew he did it, but they couldn't pin it on him, legally. I believed I could vamp him enough to make him talk, and I succeeded! I pretended to be an actress looking for a chance in movies, and let him persuade me into a screen test.

"When I finally got the proof I wanted, I slipped it into that brief case—in black and white! I was responsible for the presence of the dame you saw in Werner's compartment. My attorney has a copy of the papers in that brief case, just as a safeguard. But the boys with the stars will have possession of the original copies by now—papers that will prove beyond a doubt, that Werner is a murderer!"

Tim grabbed and pressed her hand. "Gee, what a G-man!" he exclaimed boyishly. "T a n a, I'm proud of you!"

She flushed happily. "But now that it's all over, let's just talk about—us!"

She gazed dreamily up at the low Summer moon and the scintillating pattern of gleaming stars. And Tim thought how heavenly to go romancing with this exquisitely-physical creature. But the garage entrance soon yawned just ahead, and there was no time then for love-making.

"These dizzy curves are a thrill!" Tana exclaimed, as they roared up the first steep ramp. "But why do you shift into low gear? You drive so well, I'm sure you could go up in high."

He grimaced. "Rules of the insurance people . . . cuts down the likelihood of accidents . . . anyone coming down can hear us several floor levels away, if we're in second . . . they can sound a warning. . . . There's barely enough room to pass on the levels, and they come down pretty fast, sometimes!"

Reaching Tana's roadster, they let down the top and settled themselves comfortably in the deep seat.

EXCITEMENT deepened the blue of Tana's eyes. "Let's just sit here and listen to the radio awhile," she suggested.

Tim turned the switch, and from the amplifier came the sentimental strains of "Moon Over Miami." They gazed understandingly into each other's eyes, and Tana snuggled closer. When the radio played "No Other One," Tim's arm slipped around her slender waist, and her arms went about his neck. Their lips met in a long, long kiss. The fragile strap of her gown broke, but she gave no heed. She was too deeply stirred to be aware of trivial things.

The overhead glow of the light guided Tim's exploring fingers to a soft, pliable mound of many thrills.

His pulses raced madly. He looked long into her passionate eyes, and their gaze met his with frank challenge. She raised her quivering lips again, and their sweet, crimson curves drew him irresistibly. For a blissful minute they clung, lips to lips, heart to heart. And Tim's fingers were now unleashed from all restraint. Eagerly caressing, they flew from one delightful curve of her fragrant body to another.

"Whew!" she gasped finally, pushing him gently from her. "We'd better make haste to the wide open spaces!"

Tim l a u g h e d unsteadily and started the motor. The car shot recklessly down the first ramp, the motor roaring into an ear-shattering scream. They darted around the first sharp curve, skidding dangerously.

"WHAT the hell?" Tim exclaimed, flicking off the racing engine.

"Is something wrong?" a s k e d Tana.

Tim nodded grimly. By skillful maneuvering, he managed the next curve without crashing the speeding car against a steel post, but the brake pedal was jammed to the floor, without effect, and the horn, lights—all were useless! Somewhere a brittle, crackling sound rose above the squeal of protesting tires, and its ominous, triumphant note sent shudders through tense spines.

The runaway car gained speed with each screeching curve. Tim tugged at the emergency brake, but even it refused to budge. Flashing posts at the turns looked up terrifyingly. Only sheer nerve and skill kept the swishing car on its dizzy course. No lights, no horn, no brakes! Only one hope of avoiding a disastrous crash—pray that nothing got in the way while they were racing down.

The deathlike pallor of Tim's face was Tana's proof of their plight. She leaned forward, a soft, resilient breast brushing his t e n s e arm. Thank the stars of luck that she possessed a "yen" for "extras" on cars! She was tugging on a lever that operated a special air horn, working desperately in the belief it might save them.

Tim caught the significance of her efforts, and switched on the engine to supply the necessary air. A loud blast suddenly reverberated through the building, carrying an eerie note of warning. But too late! Another car suddenly loomed in their path.

"Look out!" Tana screamed, huddling lower in her seat for protection.

Tim inched wide toward a pillar. Thank heavens! His helper, parking a car on upper three, backed into the wall with a crash! Just in time!

"Good boy!" Tim shouted, skidding deftly past.

At last the wide, open doors whirled into view. Tim swerved the berserk car out into the street—miraculously clear!—up a s t e e p grade, and bumped to a stop against the curb.

Leaping out, he ran back to the garage just in time to block Ben Turner's escape. Anger flamed in every gesture, every expression, as he glared into the brutal face of the cringing man, and in that face he read guilt!

"You dirty rat!" Tim choked. "You thought Tana would go up alone for her car—and you had orders to murder her, like you did Werner's other victims! You 'fixed' that car! But you're too late! It'll work the other way around for Werner this time! And when he hangs, you should be on a rope beside him!"

Before Turner could move, Tim dragged him out of his car and sent him sprawling on the hard concrete floor with a series of battering blows.

Turner sprang up and ran around the basement ramp, straight toward the "man lift." Tim, in hot pursuit, just missed the step on which the frightened man had leaped, but managed to grab the next one. Up they went, through the round, tapering holes in the floor.

"Keep away!" Turner yelled.

"Not until you get what's coming to you!" Tim retorted.

"You snoopy meddler," the fear-crazed man raged, "I'll kill you!"

His hoarse threat was followed by the flash of a whizzing knife dropped through the narrow opening. The keen edged blade ripped through fabric and found human flesh. But it merely grazed Tim's left shoulder.

They were almost to the top of the lift, and Turner would soon have to jump. But, suddenly, Tim felt a convulsive jerk of the heavy belt, and heard an agonized shriek of terror. He reached for the stop rope too late. He leaped to safety as Turner's mangled body fell back. The man had "gone over the top."

Tim dragged him clear of the moving lift and bent over him. Turner whispered something before he died. At sound of the commotion, a mechanic and helper had rushed up. They were just in time to hear the dying man's confession. . . .

Speeding up the broad boulevard toward Tana's a p a r t m e n t, she leaned back in the seat of the roadster, and sighed reflectively.

"You can't imagine what I went through," she said, "tolerating the caress of that old reprobate and holding him off *just enough*, while all the time I knew he had murdered my sister."

TIM patted her hand sympathetically. "Well, the whole thing is cleared up now," he soothed. "Let's just forget it all and be happy."

Tana shook off the sadness that threatened to envelop her, and as they alighted in front of her apartment house, invited Tim up for cocktails and cigarettes.

"You're thirsty, aren't you?" she asked.

"Thirsty and—starving!" he said significantly, letting his gaze roam boldly over her tempting figure.

She did not pretend to misunderstand. Her lithe body undulated, slowly, voluptuously. Her breasts seemed to swell under his admiring appraisal.

Tim swept her into his arms, his hands caressing her thrilling, pliant flesh. His shoulders hunched over her, as he bowed his head and whispered, his voice fervent with passion:

"I love you, Tana! I want you! I'm starved for you!"

"How about the night shift?" she teased.

"Let's make it a love shift!" he begged. She knew well his clean, wholesome love had been reinforced with masculine, passionate desire.

Yielding, she sought his lips in a long, flaming kiss, and nestled deeper, deeper into his arms, until their bodies were merged as one, and their souls united in rapturous satisfaction. . . .

The Broken RECORD

Was it the "voice of the other woman" that came to Marie's ears in the chill of a northwest winter?

By MARIE FORGERON

WINTER — so entrancingly beautiful, and yet so ruggedly menacing. Hollywood directors would have given much for the chance to photograph the swirling mass of flakes and to have recorded the dismal howling of the north winds.

But Hollywood has nothing to do with this story, and we find snow everywhere—a deep blanket over the face of the earth. Enormous bolls of it, like freshly picked cotton, nestling on the groaning branches and twigs of the spruce. A dizzy, blinding whirl of fleecy flakes in the air, obscuring the great opening in the forest not fifty feet from where Louie Marquis stood, which was Gull Lake, blotting out his trail back to the cabin where Marie must be even now boiling the mush for supper.

"R-r-rot-ton," hissed Louie. He was lost. He, the keenest woodsman in Little Smoky.

The blizzard had beaten him. The worst blizzard in twenty years. And such a good day! Over his shoulder was slung the freshly-skinned pelt of a silver fox. A verree, verree good day!

"By Gar," he murmured. He stumbled on, dragging his heavy, snow-shoe-laden feet. He was dog-tired. He had been traveling in beautiful circles for two hours, and getting nowhere. He was drowsy. If he could only lie down and sleep for a while. But sleep meant—

"Tam!" he exploded at the thought, and shouldered forward desperately. Suddenly a huge, black shape loomed up before him. He stopped. It was a house, a log cottage, the summer camp of people from "vay down soud"—from Hollywood, to be exact. Cold, cheerless and covered with snow.

By it Louie knew that he was yet a good three miles from home. He felt his way around to the door. He paused, jerked off his coon cap with its flaunting r a b b i t tail, scratched his head in feverish doubt. Should he try and push on to Marie and supper, and the warmth of her fine, slender young body; for his wife was beautiful, and mostly French. Or should he stay here until the blizzard had passed? He peered again through the blinding snow.

"I lose m y s e l f one t'ousand times," he spluttered.

He took off his snow-shoes, drew back and launched himself heavily against the door—once—twice. It gave. It seemed even colder inside,

Marie hastily drew a towel in front of her nude body.

but it was dry, and, Mother of Saints! there was wood, plenty of it, heaped up before the yawning fireplace. His taut face cracked into a smile. He banged shut the door, and braced a snow-shoe against it. He built a frame of sticks for a huge fire and touched a match. In a moment the leaping flames threw their dancing light about the room.

Louie squatted on the floor and held out his stiff fingers to the fire. Then he pulled from his duffelbag a small chunk of corn cake. He toasted this on a stick and gulped it down, sighing because he had no more. He filled and lighted his pipe, taking a leisurely survey of the room. It was almost bare of furniture, but on a table beneath which reposed several year-and-a-half-old movie magazines, stood a suspicious looking object reverently covered with a cloth.

Louie removed the cloth and grunted. A phonograph. He had once seen and heard one of the wonderful things at Nisswa. They had played one in a house there where the lights were dim and the girl's conversations bright; Louie recalled. Where squeaky music, dancing legs and bared breasts tried to lure the interests of trappers and hunters—to something far more exotic than snow fields.

He gazed down at the square mahogany object with profound respect. Reverently his long fingers traveled over its surface. They encountered the crank. Slowly and gently he turned it. No music came. He glanced into the interior. He saw a black disc marked with many concentric circles. Louie's sensitive fingers felt cautiously about. Something gave at their pressure, there was a low hum, and the music came. A woman's beautiful voice. A few of the words he understood—*"mon cœur . . . que j'aime . . . amour."* He hummed with the lilt of the song. His warm French nature titillated with emotion.

The music stopped and there was a grinding noise. But the disc still revolved. He gave it a perplexed look. Once more the lithe fingers explored cautiously. They touched something and the disc stopped. A moment more and he had discovered how to start it again. The music welled up to him. The melody sank into his being. He forgot the blizzard, forgot he was hungry, forgot Marie.

Yes, his wife would have been in bed long ago, and he had forgotten her. She of the wavy brown hair and the fiery, lynx-like eyes. Slender ankles, lithe fingers, fine spun features and generous, bowl-like and ivory-white breasts—so erect and alluring. Funny how fatigue from snow tires one!

Near midnight he regretfully covered the machine and carefully rolled himself in an old carpet before the fire—to dream of Marie and her warm kisses.

When he awoke in the cold, gray dawn, his first glance was toward the phonograph. He rose and beat himself warm. He lit his pipe.

THE blizzard was over. A great soft whiteness blanketed the world. He stood looking down at the phonograph, debating. Then abruptly he seized the silver fox pelt, bound it about the instrument which he wrapped in old paper, and strapped it to his back. He stepped out into the white world.

An hour later he entered his cabin. Marie was bathing, and hastily drew a towel in front of her nude body. The old wooden tub stood nearby—a half-breed Indian girl with wavy, dark brown hair, and a rather pretty oval face. Her dark eyes lighted when she saw her husband. Her hair, not quite black, set off the remarkable, clear-skinned beauty; and her nude beauty was everything that Louie could ask for. Shapely calves, shapely thighs, and a shapely abdomen dotted with an intriguingly beautiful navel; that was French-Indian Marie.

"Tam bleezard," said Louie. He stamped the snow from his boots and unslung his burden.

Marie gasped with delight at the silver fox. It meant much, much money. But the look she directed toward the phonograph was frankly perplexed. Louie set the box on the stool and adjusted its covering with infinite care. Marie could not understand her husband. Last year he had brought in a black bear pelt and it was cause for a day's celebration. This year he brought in a silver fox! And he threw it on the floor!

Louie pointed a long finger at the covered box, then at Marie. "No touch heem!"

She bowed her head and went back to the stove.

Louie sat down and ate prodigiously of corn cakes and bacon, washed down with huge cups of black coffee. He lighted his pipe and puffed for half an hour. Then he rose, stretched lazily, and started on the day's round of the traps.

That evening after supper Louie u n c o v e r e d the phonograph. He placed it on the floor, and the music came. He squatted cross-legged near it, and presently began to sway gently to the rhythm. When the first burst of sound smote her ears, Marie, silent in her corner, drew in her breath sharply, so sharply she was afraid Louie might have heard it even above the music. He reached over to his shapely young wife, and she trembled as he took her in his arms for a kiss. Their warm lips met in a scorching kiss d u r i n g which time her tiny red tongue drove between his shining, ivory teeth and sent thrills shivering up and down his spinal column. Louie *did* love her, and he liked to be kissed just like that. Her young breasts heaved passionately,—more so as he drew away to sit down nearby.

Her husband, h e r m a n , had brought the voice of a strange woman into the house. Eee-yah, a voice laden with love. And there he sat, charmed at the melody of it. Such a voice must have a beautiful owner —soft, white, gentle, unlike herself.

When the log in the air-tight had burned to a smouldering red mass, Louie replaced the phonograph on the stool. She knew he wanted her; might soon be in the strong, muscular arms of her husband . . . yet what about that voice. Louie's voice interrupted her reverie; she turned.

"Bed," he said.

Marie raised her chin almost imperceptibly toward the phonograph. "What ees?" she asked.

"Devil—ma petite," he boomed with a great laugh, crushing her to him. The next night, and the next, and the next—all evening the voice in the box sang to Louie, swaying cross-legged on the floor. And Marie sat still in her corner. Louie's usual after-supper occupations were neglected and forgotten—the gun cleaning, repairing the traps, tightening the snow-shoe thongs, solitaire with the greasy pack of cards. His pipe even was filled but once or twice.

ONE still noon, Marie tiptoed breathlessly to the box, with infinite caution lifted its cover. She waited a moment, and then tremblingly lifted its lid. Nothing happened.

She peered within blankly. She saw nothing soft or gentle or beautiful—nothing that could make such a voice. Only bright metal and a black round thing, like a large, thin, flat cake, burned to a crisp. She lowered her fingers toward this cake-like thing and drew t h e m quickly back. But a second time, with great courage, she touched it. Nothing happened. She felt of its edge. It was brittle, like dried reindeer or walrus bone.

Hot thoughts raged through her mind with the memory of that voice. Little did she know the woman was only a Hollywood "talkie" star, and that the one little black disc represented a couple of cents royalty to the singer. She tiptoed to a shelf and returned, grasping a h e a v y knife with a short blunt blade. Suddenly she plunged it downward. There was a sharp, snapping sound, and the black, cake-like thing broke in two pieces.

Marie lowered the lid of the box, replaced the cover as she had found it and went about her work.

After supper, L o u i e as usual placed the box on the floor and opened it. Marie's eyes contracted and her fingers moved almost imperceptibly in her lap a s s h e watched him. Suddenly he stiffened, remained so an instant, sprang to his feet.

"Gr-r-r-r!"

He wheeled and jerked her to her feet. He raised his right arm. She lowered her head for the blow. But he did not strike.

"So—you do as you tam pleez-z, no mattair what I z-zay!"

He shook her and pushed her from him, and in so doing his rough hands grazed her bosom, sending a thrill racing through her body as the breasts and the nipples stiffened. She loved her man, this French-Indian girl!

But Marie cowered in her corner, rubbing the arm he had held in a steely, vise-like and masculine grip.

Louie squatted on the floor with the two pieces of disc on his knee. He scratched his head. Then placing them flat on the floor he fitted the broken edges together and with infinite pains bound a buckskin thong about their rim. He replaced the disc in the machine and turned to Marie with a soft, insinuating smile.

"Heh—you—jealous of my singing bird? I will have her sing for you some more."

He started the phonograph, and the music came. But such music. Each time the needle struck the crack in the disc there was a rasping sound, a razor-edged cachination. And when it reached the place where the knife had penetrated it wailed and sputtered intolerably. The beautiful voice had changed as if by a miracle into the crackling of a quarrelsome hag. Louie stopped the phonograph with an oath.

But Marie, silent in her corner, her young breasts trembling tumultuously, was jubilant.

The Wasp

(*Concluded from page* 51)

are a thousand along Wilshire Boulevard who'd be nice to me if I just batted an eyelid!"

No, there wasn't much surprise when Madelynn left Ben's house.

Ben Fleet went out of pictures. He could not fight his wife. He would not defend himself.

"All my life," he tells his friends, "I have wanted a son. All my life, ever since I can remember. And now I have a son — and it is torture."

Hundreds of butterflies come each day to Hollywood. Some of them die in a day. But who cares for that? There are always butterflies. And hundreds of wasps come into Hollywood each day. And they live, and grow fat. And a world of fans adores them. For they have *not* as yet scorched their lovely and frail wings.

Tropical Intrigue

A local feud breaks up the "action" of an "on location" picture colony

By ANDRÉ SURDOS

SAM DOUGLAS pounded down the steep slope toward where the white puff of smoke still lingered. The resultant echoes of the shot reached his ears in magnified proportion. His thoughts were keeping pace with him.

More trouble with the native cast, he guessed. The Indians and Colombians were a motley crew. They'd made trouble ever since he started shooting three months ago. And the hell of it was—he couldn't discover a reason for it! Once again he cursed the Hollywood big-wigs who had insisted on shooting the picture in the tropics.

A milling press filled the clearing when he broke through the trees. He elbowed through to where a man lay flat on his back, his face pale beneath its heavy tan. The open shirtfront revealed a bullet wound in the fleshy part of the shoulder. Douglas knelt and probed with his finger, then his glare went about the sullen ring of faces.

"No bones broken, Kelly," he said at last, helping his ace cameraman to his feet. He supported him into the rude office building and eased him into a chair.

Kelly's face assumed a natural hue as his chief cauterized and bound his wound.

"I was walking about the clearing when a bullet laid me out, Sam. I had the boys put Salvador in a makeshift hoosegow, just in case."

Douglas snorted. "That's the fellow who started the last ruckus!" He went to the door and barked an order. Presently the half-caste was shoved into the room where he stood with sullen indifference.

"I make trouble you no let me go!" he threatened.

Douglas smiled grimly. No amount of punishment would ever change this fellow's attitude. But he'd have given a lot to know what was going on behind that thick skull.

"Salvador," he said slowly, "we've tried to treat you and your fellow workers decently. You get good wages and food, and your sleeping quarters are better than any you've ever had. Yet you start trouble. Why? It never gets you anywhere."

A cunning light flickered in the shifty eyes.

"Americans steal gold from mine —do not give to owner!"

Douglas was impatient. "How can

that be—when this mine is worked out? We paid the Colombian Government for the use of a locale, we're not after treasure."

Only the flexing of the caste's powerful fingers betrayed his emotion. "You steal gold—belong to us!" he repeated, stolidly.

Douglas controlled his rising ire. "Who hired you to start all this trouble?"

Salvador refused to speak, waited stolidly for the sentence he knew would come.

"I'm sure that you shot Mr. Kelly!" Douglas said. "You've got one hour to pack and get off this property. And—*don't come back!*"

AN HOUR later Douglas and Kelly were on the porch when Salvador was escorted to the clearing's edge. As his arms were released, he shook his fists and shouted threats.

Sam Douglas mounted the horse that was brought to him. Kelly's look fixed on the director's gunbelt. "Good hunting," he said, waving from where he sat.

Steaming mist rose from the dank underbrush as Douglas followed the dusky jungle trail. Swarms of gnats stung at him. He wished it were possible to make colored movies of the brilliantly plumaged macaws and toucans that fluttered through the trees.

Soon his mind returned to his troubles. Filming costs were mounting daily. He wasn't a third through, yet he had exceeded his budget. That might mean his job when he returned to Hollywood.

His horse shied suddenly and saved him from the huge boa that dropped from above. As he rode on, he kept more on the alert. Dusk found him near the hut of a native

known to him. Juan Castrillo gladly put him up for the night. Sunrise found him on the trail again. It was nearly noon when the gleaming white-towered cathedral of Medellin appeared in the distance.

The bank was his first stop. Senor de Santos was glad to see him. An excellent cigar and a most refreshing drink mellowed Douglas somewhat. After a few pleasantries, he made known his errand.

"You know, of course, all about our labor troubles, senor. I'm at a loss to explain them and thought you might be able to shed some light on the mystery." The American studied the many-chinned face of the banker.

De Santos smoked thoughtfully, the while he studied Douglas keenly. "I have an idea, senor," he admitted, "but I hesitate to say anything that might cast reflections on good friends of mine. Yet I must consider you and your company. They do much business with my bank. Let me begin by telling you a story. A wealthy Colombian once owned the mine that you now lease. He was a motion-picture producer, too. Reverses took most of his wealth and he borrowed money from your company. Most unfortunately, he was bitten by the deadly *fer de lance,* and died. Soon his wife died, and the children—a boy and a girl—were too young to carry on. Your company absorbed his picture company. The children have always believed that their father was murdered and the property taken from them." The banker's face was sorrowful as he added: "I have been unable to persuade them they are wrong."

"Tell me their names," insisted Douglas. "I'll go and see them, make them see how mistaken they are."

De Santos put out a hand in protest. "No! They might harm you —then I would feel responsible."

"It's a chance I must take," insisted Douglas. "If you won't tell me their names, I'll find out elsewhere. I know the story."

The banker shrugged his resignation.

"Very well then. But I wash my hands of all responsibility. The name is Dominguez. Here—" and he wrote something on the back of a card—"is their address."

DOUGLAS banged the huge knocker on the wooden gate. A barefoot servant barred his way. He flung a Colombian dollar on the

grass at her feet. As she stooped, he strode into the garden.

He appreciated the setting. Lovely flowers bloomed everywhere, and a river edged one end of the grounds. It was lined with trees from which lavender blossoms trailed in the slow current. What a shot it would be!

A fer de lance slithered from the scattered paper.

He was attracted to two persons seated at a table beneath a huge umbrella. They watched his approach in silence. He guessed who they were and spoke first in self defense.

"You are the Senorita Rosita Dominguez?" He bowed.

She inclined her head. Her lovely face remained tranquil as her dark eyes probed deep into his gray ones.

"I think," she said calmly, "that you must be the American picture director."

Douglas nodded quickly. "That's right. I came to see if I might not convince you how wrong you are about my company. Senor de Santos told me how you feel."

"Did he tell you that my father had the money in his pocket to pay off the loan when the snake bit him? It was gone when his body was found!"

He hadn't known that. "You think my company is responsible for that?" he questioned gravely.

She shrugged, and the movement caused her full breasts to sway deliciously. For the first time her femininity impressed him.

"What else am I to think, senor? An Indian saw a white man place that snake in my father's room."

"That doesn't prove the white man was connected with my company."

"We have nothing to gain," put in the young brother, "by arguing, my sister." His eyes flashed.

"Go into the house, Manuel, I will settle this—alone."

The lad obeyed without a word, reached the front door. His terrified scream brought Douglas running. His gun leaped from its holster! The shot beheaded a deadly *fer de lance*, left it writhing in the grass! The girl's hands clutched the American's arms.

"Thank you, senor," she murmured brokenly. "My brother means more than life to me."

She did not withdraw her hands as he possessed them. Her brother, trembling from his narrow escape, allowed the servant woman to lead him into the house.

"I feel that you are our friend," said Rosita, pulling him to the bench beside her. "We have need for one in whom we can confide. I was attending school in America when father died. I came home at once. Things were in a terrible state. Had it not been for the kindness of Senor de Santos, father's old friend, I don't know what we would have done. But now he—"

"Yes," prompted Douglas.

"He—he wants me to marry him."

DOUGLAS was thoughtful. "Senor de Santos is a fine man, but too old for you. If I read you correctly, you need romance. You dream of the time when you will meet a man who will save you from a terrible danger. I know, for my own sister is like that."

She was long silent and he asked a question.

"Are you responsible for the labor trouble I am having?"

She met his gaze, and the blank look in her eyes was an answer without words.

"What do you mean, senor?"

He told her of the difficulty he had in filming the scenes he must take before he could return to Hollywood. He also told of the attempt to kill his cameraman. But he did not say that the banker had hinted that she and her brother were guilty.

Before she could reply, her brother came running from the house, greatly excited. "Rosita! The snake the senor killed must be the one I had in the cage in my room. It is empty!"

Douglas looked inquiringly at the girl.

"Senor de Santos raises snakes to get the toxins with which to combat their poisonous bites," she explained. "Manuel bothered him until he gave him a *fer de lance.*"

"May I see the box in which the snake was kept?" requested Douglas, and followed after them into the big house. He examined the box closely. The front was hinged at the bottom. At the top he saw something he did not immediately reveal to them. Then he returned the box to her.

Presently Rosita asked him into the patio. They were served with cooling drinks and left alone. The low chair in which she sat brought her knees to a higher level than her hips and Douglas had a glimpse of her lovely white thighs. As he got up to place his glass on the table, she bent over to tie her shoe lace. He saw cinnamon-centered mounds of perfection. Without volition his hand reached forward and cupped a lovely beacon.

For a moment he thought she meant to fight, then the swell of her breast told him she had awakened at his touch. She came erect at his pull. Her arms went about his neck and she quivered as his hands went over the lush curves of her hips. She trembled in ecstacy.

Step by step he backed her to a wicker couch and bent her down to its cover. His hand slid over her skirt. She drove him almost to distraction with the mad movement of her tongue in his dry mouth. Together they two rose almost to the sublimely beautiful heights of passion and love denied. . . .

A T THE BANK, much later, he told de Santos of the snake incident. The banker became highly excited.

"Why did I give in to that boy's whim?" he cried.

"Don't worry about it," laughed Douglas. "That particular snake is in snake heaven—if there is such a thing."

De Santos failed to join the levity. "You like the senorita and her brother, yes?"

"I never saw a more lovely girl, she's the equal of any star in Hollywood. And the boy is nice, too."

The banker's eyes flickered with an undefined emotion, then became expressionless. "She is very charming," he agreed, "that is why I chose her for my wife. You will treat this as confidential?" Without waiting for a reply, he went on: "By what trail are you returning to the mine?"

"I hadn't thought," replied the surprised Douglas. "However, I only know one way, so I shall take that one."

"Be careful," warned de Santos. "The snakes are alive after dusk."

Douglas smiled. "The snake incident has upset your nerves, senor. I will stop at Juan Castrillo's tonight. You know him?"

"But slightly," admitted de Santos indifferently. He offered his pudgy hand. "I pray that you will not meet with the misfortune that attended Senor Dominguez."

As Sam Douglas rode away, he wondered if the banker were inwardly as sincere as his words. He knew the girl had not favored his suit—yet.

* * * * *

It was after ten when Douglas reached Castrillo's hut. After eating, he threw himself on the bed, fully clothed. Tired out, sleep soon claimed him.

A slight rustling sound half aroused him. It sounded again and filled him with dread! He kept rigidly still, hoping his dread thought was wrong. Something smooth and cold and wriggling touched his left hand, sent a shiver throughout his being.

Thankful that he had not undressed, he used his right hand to cautiously ease the knife from his belt sheath. His fingers closed about the bone haft, convulsively.

His eyes had accustomed themselves to the gloom. He could see the reared head of the snake. It was a *fer de lance!* Its beady eyes fixed unblinkingly on him. Cold clammy sweat beaded his forehead. His hands were drenched, his nerves near the breaking point!

Suddenly, he jerked his body to one side and slashed at the reptile! The slimy thing writhed over his body. Sam Douglas saw a red splotch on his arm, and fell into a half coma.

Daylight streamed through the square window opening when he came to himself. The snake lay beside him, motionless. His swipe had completely severed the head. Douglas staggered to his feet, his nerves still quivery. Close scrutiny of the wound in his arm filled him with heartfelt relief. What he had thought to be a snake bite was a cut inflicted by his own knife.

WHEN he went into the other room of that hut, he stopped short in surprise. Castrillo lay in one corner, bound and gagged. Douglas freed him.

"What happened, Juan?"

The Colombian shook his head in bewilderment. "I do not know, senor.

I see nothing, hear nothing, knowing nothing till I wake up tied and with something stuffed in mouth." He felt the back of his head. "It hurts —here."

Douglas examined the lump on Juan's head. No wonder he knew nothing. He had been knocked unconscious while asleep. They went outside and circled the hut. Outside the window to his room, the American discovered footprints, but they told him nothing. The mosquito netting had been slit. The snake had been thrust through the window.

Before continuing his journey, Douglas gave Castrillo instructions that made the native smile grimly. The trip to the mine was without event, and Kelly's report was merely routine.

*   *   *   *   *

Visitors came while several scenes were being shot the next day. And Sam Douglas immediately used the newcomers in a short closeup. He'd make the big-wigs in Hollywood sputter and make the wires red-hot. That's how sure he was that Rosita would wow them. Hard up, were they? Well—he'd start the Dominguez family on the uptrend once more.

Loquacious Kelly was overcome by the girl's beauty, and cast sly glances at his boss. After a tour of inspection, the girl asked for permission to address the native extras. Douglas was dubious, a little uneasy, but gave in. She spoke to them in Spanish, which he understood.

"Some of you formerly worked for my father when he operated this mine and made pictures. The American Film Company took over his interests legally. Yet some one has stirred you up against them, has been feeding you insidious tales.

There is no gold to be found here. Won't you be loyal to the company that pays you such fine wages—to Mr. Douglas, your director?"

The men cheered and went to their quarters, and Douglas could tell they were more carefree than at any time since he had hired them. He escorted the girl to his office and expressed himself with feeling.

"That was a great speech, senorita. I don't know why you did it, feeling as you do about—"

"I did it for you," she confessed, flushing a bit. "Manuel and I want to prove that we had nothing to do with your troubles here."

Then Kelly and her brother entered the room.

"I am going to stay and work for Mr. Douglas!" enthused the lad. "Senor Kelly has promised to make a cameraman of me."

Rosita paled. "But I—I can't stay in Medellin alone, Manuel," she faltered.

"You could stay here," suggested Manuel. "I'm sure Mr. Douglas will give you a part in his picture."

Kelly winked slyly at Douglas who relieved her embarrassment.

"I've a two room cottage here, remain here for the night. We'll talk things over in the morning. I really believe your brother should have his chance. Think it over tonight."

A PIERCING SCREAM snapped Sam Douglas from his bed to the floor. The luminous alarm dial told him it was four a. m. Slipping quickly into trousers and boots, he grabbed his automatic and went out into the night.

He was sure that Rosita had uttered that scream, and cursed himself for letting her have his room. Kelly joined him in the clearing.

Many of their cast were up, stirring.

"Get them back to bed, Kelly," Douglas ordered, feeling certain he could handle the situation. The cottage door was locked, but gave under his onslaught.

A whimpering sound reached his ears as he half fell inside, then he felt a soft body against his. The girl's thinly covered breasts warmed his chest. Her curves molded to him, quivered there. He tried to quiet her nerves. Finally his murmured endearments and soft kisses awakened a response. At last she tried to explain her scream.

"I—I heard a snake on the floor!"

Quick as a flash he picked her up and sat her on top of a wall shelf. A match flickered and he touched flame to the wick of an oil lamp. Rosita flushed and tried to hide her near-nudeness. Douglas grabbed a robe from the bed, flung it at her.

A pounding sounded on the connecting door and Manuel's excited calls came to them. Douglas warned him to wait and went on with his methodical search of the room. He found nothing and was about convinced she had imagined the snake when he spied a banana crate beneath the window. It was nearly filled with refuse paper. He kicked it over and stepped back with ready-held automatic.

A *fer de lance* slithered from the scattered paper! A sharp crack sounded, and the snake writhed in death throes. Douglas kicked it out the door and called to Manuel to go back to bed. Lifting Rosita from her precarious perch, he placed her on the bed. She clung to him, gave him kiss for kiss, in utter abandon.

"I'll stand guard outside until daylight," he whispered, freeing himself with difficulty. Blowing out the

light, he went outside to sit on the stoop.

"Better go to bed, Kelly," he advised, when the young cameraman came up to him. "That shoulder of your isn't well yet, you know."

Douglas hadn't been long alone when he felt a slight touch on his back. He turned his head, saw the wraith-like figure of Rosita in the doorway. She beckoned him into the room, smiling alluringly.

As one in a daze he got up and entered the house. Hardly was the door closed when she was in his arms. The urge of her passion quickly communicated itself to him. His busy hands caressed her charms. Her twin breasts pulsed frantically under his caresses. They were ripe as passion fruit and sweet. She panted desperately as his lips kissed the downy hollow between her mol-lescent mounds.

It was mid-morning when two figures emerged from the forest and came across the clearing. Rosita, Manuel, Kelly and Douglas watched from their seats on the office porch.

DOUGLAS recognized Juan Castrillo and the trouble maker, Estaban Salvador. The former employee walked as though in dread of the huge banana knife wielded by Juan. As they neared the porch, a horseman rode toward them from another direction. But Douglas paid little attention to the Senor de Santos.

"Where'd you find him?" he asked Juan.

"Heading away from here with an empty snake cage in his hand."

The American nodded grimly. "That settles it! There's no doubt that he put the snake in the senorita's room."

"The senorita's room!" echoed the banker, his face pasty.

"Yes. They stayed here last night and Kelly and I gave up our quarters to them. I imagine Salvador thought he was putting the snake in my room."

After a moment's silence, he went on: "We captured the snake. The best punishment I know of is to put him in the room with it."

Salvador lost his stolidity, paled. "I will tell!" he screamed.

A shot sounded and the man fell! Douglas turned to the livid-faced banker, took the smoking gun from his hand.

"You should not have done that, senor. We were about to learn something."

Color slowly came back to de Santos' flabby cheeks. "Perhaps not," he admitted, "but in Colombia we do things differently than you do in America. The thought of that dog placing a snake in the senorita's room maddened me. He will never harm another!"

Douglas nodded grimly. "Things are different here. We do not have snake charmers in America, save in the side shows. Nor do we have supposed samaritans who save the lives of many but take the lives of a few who stand in the way of their ambitions!"

De Santos turned thoughtful eyes on the American.

"You mean there are people like that—in Colombia?" His tone was silky soft.

Rosita shuddered. "Could anyone be so cruel?"

"Do you know who it is, Sam?" queried Kelly.

Douglas nodded. "He is—look out!" he warned. De Santos had snatched Kelly's gun, was aiming at the girl. Douglas fumbled for his own, knew he was too late. The banker's finger was tensing on the trigger.

Snatching the banana knife from Juan, Douglas gave it a desperate underhanded sling. The wicked weapon hurtled through the air and nearly severed the man's arm above the elbow! De Santos screamed horribly and clutched at the gushing wound. Kelly and Castrillo rushed him into the office to apply a tourniquet.

Douglas led Rosita into the cottage and sat her on the bed.

"I suspected de Santos after examining the snake box he gave your brother. Gum was all that had held it fast. When that dried the snake was soon free. He wanted Manuel out of the way. During that night he actually attempted to get me, too.

"I sent Juan to keep tab on Salvador. He overheard the two plotting my death. I pulled the stall about putting Salvador in the room with the snake so he'd confess and implicate the banker. He did!"

"You think de Santos killed my father?"

"I can answer that," said Kelly, who had come from the office in time to hear her question. "He confessed before he died. It was he who caused your father to invest unwisely. He killed your father and took the money. I think, with the signed confession I got, that you'll get some of your property back."

Douglas and Rosita were looking at one another. Kelly grinned and left them alone. The picture director took her small hand in his.

"I was thinking of getting you into pictures," he ventured after a long silence. "With your beauty and —and form you can go far."

She got up and stood in front of him. She stood there for a moment, letting his eyes drink their fill of her glorious beauty.

"Talkies" of Criminals

SPEAKING motion picture films of criminals and dangerous felons, made available throughout the country when an important search is on, is an idea originated by Colonel H. Norman Schwarzkopf, superintendent of the New Jersey State police. This idea is shortly to be made operative through the perfection of a device that dispenses with the services of sound technicians and will permit an ordinary intelligent policeman to operate it. It bids fair to revolutionize methods of recognizing desperadoes.

For purposes of detection there is all the difference in the world between viewing stock photos of criminals with their Bertillon measurements and seeing the criminals in action and hearing their voices in response to questions. Obviously the latter method of identification is more expensive. But escapes of dangerous prisoners and the too frequent persistence in lives of crime by men and women who have been paroled or have served out their sentences amply justify the difference in cost by the measure of protection it throws over society.

Not every offender, of course, need be subjected to the process, which has met with approbation in police circles wherever it has been explained. The Department of Justice at Washington might operate as a clearing house for these films by the maintenance of a "library" of them for temporary distribution wherever needed.

The plan has the approval and support of "SAUCY MOVIE TALES" monthly magazine.

If, as Colonel Schwarzkopf says, a much-wanted criminal knew that talking pictures were shown of him at principal moving picture theatres the country over as well as in all central police bureaus, that fact would go a long way to break down his morale. Crime, in other words, would become a much more dangerous business to its perpetrator.

Success in Three Easy Lessons